The Escape of the Plant That Ate Dirty Socks

NANCY MCARTHUR'S first published writing was in her school newpaper. She starts writing a book with "a very messy rough draft. Then I revise the whole thing two or three times." Her first two Avon Camelot books about Michael and Norman are *The Plant That Ate Dirty Socks* and *The Return of the Plant That Ate Dirty Socks*. The fourth one will be published in July 1993. Her other books for younger readers are *Megan Gets a Dollhouse, Pickled Peppers, The Adventure of the Buried Treasure,* and *The Adventure of the Backyard Sleepout.* Ms. McArthur lives in Berea, Ohio, a suburb of Cleveland. She has a lot of plants, but none of them has eaten anything—so far.

The Escape of the Plant That Ate Dirty Socks

Nancy McArthur

AN AUTHORS GUILD BACKINPRINT.COM EDITION

The Escape of the Plant That Ate Dirty Socks

AN AUTHORS GUILD BACKINPRINT.COM EDITION
Published by iUniverse, Inc.

For information address:
iUniverse, Inc.
2021 Pine Lake Road, Suite 100
Lincoln, NE 68512
www.iuniverse.com

Originally published by Avon Camelot

ISBN: 0-595-32123-2

Printed in the United States of America

To the world's best sister, brother, and sister-in-law:
Susan Lee McArthur
John Palmer McArthur
Barbara Berg McArthur

Special thanks to: Pat Berg, Karen Kotrba, Erica Luoma, Todd Linton, Margy Dwyer, Pat Jenkins, Jan C. Snow, Barb Koepen, Sue Lazuda, Ellen Krieger, John and Ruby Martin, Chris Frost, Scott Woodward, Sue Kennel Hall, Mollie Buckley, Mike and Andy Sparks, the Rolland family.

Chapter 1

"Don't panic," mumbled Michael sleepily. Then he got so tangled up in his blankets that he fell right out of bed and hit the rug with a thump.

His younger brother Norman, the expert pest, had just waked him before dawn to tell him that their weird giant sock-eating pet plants had disappeared from their room.

"Did you look out in the hall?" asked Michael as he rolled around on the floor trying to get out of his blanket cocoon.

"Yeah, but they're not out there," replied Norman. "Besides, they couldn't get out of here without us pushing them on their skateboards."

Michael sighed. He and Norman had fought many battles with their parents to be allowed to keep their plants, which they had grown from seeds that Michael had ordered by mail. But the plants had caused one uproar after another. It hadn't been easy trying to keep them out of trouble.

Michael knew that there were always going to be strange problems with plants that picked up socks with their long powerful vines late at night, sucked them in through ice-cream-cone-shaped leaves, and then burped. But he'd never expected them to vanish. He tried to calm down and think clearly.

His plant Stanley, the bigger one, ate only dirty socks, while Norman's plant Fluffy ate only clean ones. But lately Stanley had also developed a liking for orange juice, and Fluffy appeared to enjoy it, too.

"Let's check the kitchen," Michael said, finally freeing himself. "Stanley's gotten refrigerator doors open before to get at juice."

Norman asked, "Didn't you give him some last night?"

"No, Mom said we only had enough for breakfast, so she wouldn't let me."

"But how could they get to the kitchen?"

Michael had no idea, so he didn't reply. He just headed down the hall, with Norman following.

In the dark dining room the boys saw a dim light glowing from the kitchen. Michael stopped to listen, and Norman bumped into him. They heard something rustling.

Slowly reaching out from the door came a long, leafy vine. It waved around like an elephant's trunk looking for peanuts.

Michael stood still, curious to see what it would do next. The vine stretched out, touched a chair leg, wrapped itself around it, and pulled. The chair whisked away, into the kitchen. They heard it thump on the floor in there.

Norman darted past Michael, but Michael grabbed him by the back of his pajama top. "Wait," he whispered. "Here it comes again. Let's see what happens."

The long, leafy vine snaked out, touched another chair, and tugged. When the chair moved a little, the

2

vine let go. It tried a leg of the large, heavy table. This time the furniture did not move, but the plant did. Gripping the table, Stanley slowly rolled himself out of the kitchen.

"Wow!" exclaimed Norman.

Stanley let go of the table leg and reached into the hall to find something else to grab. Michael was amazed that his plant could pull itself along this way. When they had fastened the plants to skateboards so it would be easier to move them and turn them to face the sun, he never dreamed that they would learn how to move around by themselves.

From the kitchen they heard another thump. The boys looked in. The light came from the open refrigerator. Fluffy was trying to use the chair that Stanley had yanked into the room. But all he could do was drag it, thumping and bumping around the floor.

Norman rushed in to help Fluffy. Michael followed Stanley to see what he was going to do next.

On the kitchen floor lay an empty plastic juice pitcher and tiny orange puddles. Norman thought Fluffy looked tired and upset. He was always thrilled when his plant learned to do something new, but now he just wanted to get him back to the room and maybe sing to him to calm him down. Norman's singing had the opposite effect on everyone else, but Fluffy seemed to like it.

But first, because he was a neatness nut, Norman quickly put the chair back, turned on the ceiling light, closed the refrigerator, wiped up the puddles with paper towels, and put the pitcher in the sink.

He turned around just in time to see Fluffy wrapping a vine around a drawer handle. He jumped for it, but not fast enough. The drawer flew out and crashed, scattering knives, forks, and spoons.

3

Fluffy looked shaken. Norman threw his arms around his plant. "It's all right," he said soothingly. "It's not your fault. I'll roll you back to our room. I can pick this stuff up later." Fluffy touched Norman's head with one vine and put another around his shoulder.

Out in the hall Michael was fascinated with the way Stanley was slowly moving along. He thought that Dr. Sparks, the plant expert they had met on their Florida vacation, would really be amazed if she found out about this.

As Stanley reached the door of the boys' room, the door across the hall opened and Mom came out.

"Are you all right?" she asked. "I thought I heard sort of a crash. Where are you going with your plant?"

At the other end of the hall Norman appeared, pushing Fluffy.

"Okay, what's going on?" demanded Mom.

Norman replied, "I have to go to the bathroom."

She asked, "Then why are you wheeling your plant around?"

"Fluffy has to go, too," said Norman. He rolled his plant right past her into the bathroom and shut the door.

"What are you two up to?" asked Mom. "What was that noise I heard?"

Michael replied, "It sounded like it came from the kitchen."

"And Norman and Fluffy were coming from the kitchen?" she asked. "The plants are up to something, aren't they? They usually are when we have uproars in the middle of the night!"

Just then Dad, squinting sleepily, joined the hallway meeting. "What's going on?" he asked.

As Michael tried to think how to break the news to them without making Mom ballistic, they heard the

4

toilet flush. The bathroom door opened, and Fluffy came out.

Dad looked horrified. Then the plant got closer and he glimpsed Norman behind it, pushing.

"Good grief!" exclaimed Dad. "For a second there, I thought I was still asleep and dreaming that Fluffy was running around by himself."

Mom remarked, "What a nightmare that would be!" She turned to the boys, standing next to their plants. "Okay, no more stalling, guys. What's really going on?"

As if in answer to her question, Stanley reached a vine into the boys' room. Then, with no one touching him, he rolled out of the hall. They all crowded into the doorway, watching the plant return to its usual spot beside Michael's bed.

"This is the last straw!" yelled Mom. "We can't have these plants running around loose!"

Michael protested, "But they only went to the kitchen to get orange juice. If we give them some every night, they won't want to go anywhere."

Norman added, "They were trying to come back to the room on their own. They weren't just running around for no reason. Actually they weren't even running. They were going really slow. Rolling to the kitchen isn't easy when you're a plant!"

Dad asked, "Did they get the juice?"

"Yeah," answered Norman. "But I cleaned up the mess. Except for knives and forks and spoons all over the floor. We better wash those before we put them back."

"Knives!" exclaimed Mom, looking alarmed. "What were they doing with those?"

"Nothing," explained Norman. "The drawer came out and dumped them. It was an accident."

Mom concluded, "That must have been the crash I heard."

"It was a big one," agreed Norman. He began to giggle. Behind him, Fluffy was tickling him to get attention.

"See?" said Norman. "Fluffy wants to go back in the room. He doesn't want to run all over the house." The others moved out of the way so Norman could push Fluffy back next to his bed.

"Don't worry," Michael told Mom. "I'm sure they'll stay put from now on, as long as we give them juice."

"You'd better be right," said Mom sternly. "I don't want to get up in the morning and find them in the kitchen fixing socks for breakfast."

As he was trying to go back to sleep, Michael reached for Stanley to pat his leaves, but he didn't have to reach far. As he turned his head, some leaves on the pillow tickled his nose.

Chapter 2

At breakfast Michael felt cranky from not enough sleep. He was in no mood for ultimatums from his parents about the latest plant problem. But he knew they would probably be starting any minute.

He hacked his banana into messy chunks and chomped glumly on his cereal. Across from him Norman was doing what always drove Michael crazy. He neatly sliced his banana into little circles exactly the same thickness. Then he spaced them evenly around on top of his cereal and ate them one at a time.

"Why do you always have to do that?" snarled Michael. "It takes you practically all day!"

Norman glared at him. "I like my food to be neat," he replied grumpily. "Not like yours."

"So what!" said Michael. "It all gets smooshed together when it goes down your gullet."

Dad said, "The way Norman eats is not the problem. Now that we know it's possible for your plants to move around on their own, it's even more important that we don't let any more grow with unsuspecting families all over town. We have to make sure that you get back all the seeds that Jason sold at school while we were away on vacation.''

Dad turned to Mom. ''And we'll have to get back the plant your mother is growing from that cutting she took from Stanley.''

Mom replied, ''She's too far away for us to go pick it up. Maybe I could persuade her just to use some weed killer on it. But first I have to figure out how to break the news to her about what that plant will do when it gets bigger.''

Dad turned back to Michael. ''I want you to find out from Jason today who he sold seeds to and then talk to every kid who bought one to make sure we get them all back.''

Michael put his head in his hands. ''How can I explain to kids why they can't keep their seeds?'' he asked. ''And I don't ever want to talk to Jason again.''

Dad insisted, ''You'll have to work it out. This is your responsibility.''

''Yeah,'' added Norman bossily. ''They're seeds from your plant.''

Michael whined, ''But I don't know what to say to him!''

Dad instructed, ''Walk right up to him and say 'hi.' Then tell him I said you have to get every one of those seeds back or he'll have to answer to me.''

Slumping in his chair, Michael stared into his milk. This was not going to be a good day. He wished he could go back to bed and start over.

Michael would rather have taken a math test than talk to Jason. Just the day before he and Norman had got back at Jason for selling the seeds by siccing the plants on him and getting orange juice all over him, so he was pretty sure Jason wouldn't want to talk to him either. But if he had to do it, he decided he'd better get it over with. At recess, he got up his nerve and walked over to Jason.

"Hi, my dad says you have to get back all the seeds, or else," he said.

"That wasn't the deal yesterday," replied Jason. "You said just pay back the kids on the waiting list for seeds and buy back seeds from anybody who wanted their money back. You didn't say all!"

"My dad says all," insisted Michael.

Jason was staring down at his shoes instead of looking Michael in the eye. He looked as if he felt so guilty that Michael was almost sorry for him, even though the whole mess had happened because Jason had helped himself to the seeds without Michael knowing.

Michael asked, "Have you talked to anybody yet?"

"I was going to at lunch," Jason answered. "Most of them aren't going to want to sell back their seeds."

"How many did you sell?"

"Fifteen. Sixteen. Maybe a couple more."

Michael said, "You have to remember them all." Jason looked so discouraged that Michael offered, "I know Chad got one. I can talk to him. If you make a list, we could divide it up and each talk to half."

"Okay," said Jason, looking up at last.

Michael went to find Chad. "You know that seed Jason sold you?" he said.

Chad answered, "If I knew you didn't know he had them, I wouldn't have paid him. I would have waited till you got back from Florida and paid you. He's giving you the money, isn't he?"

Michael explained, "He was going to go halves with me, but my folks said we have to get all the seeds back, so he's going to give all the money back."

Chad said, "Mine isn't a seed anymore. It's already started to grow, so I'll just keep it."

"How about double your money back?"

"No, I want a plant like yours and Norman's."

"Triple?"

"I'll think about it," Chad said.

After school Michael asked Jason, "Have you got the list done yet?"

"I'll do it tonight," promised Jason.

"Okay, I'll call you after dinner to get the names."

On his way home from school Norman stopped to talk to their neighbor Mrs. Smith, who was working in her yard. A small, shaggy brown dog Norman had never seen before was running around her.

"Where did you get that dog?" he asked.

"At the animal shelter last week," she replied. She called to the dog, "Margo, sit!" Margo sat down immediately.

Norman stroked the dog's silky back. "How did you get her to do that?" he asked.

"I took her to a dog training class and learned how to get her to behave on command. She's a quick learner."

Norman asked, "Do they have a plant training class?"

"You say the funniest things," said Mrs. Smith with a grin. "Look at what else Margo can do." She picked up an old tennis ball and tossed it away. "Margo, fetch!" she called. The dog galloped after the ball, picked it up with her mouth, and sat down.

"Bring it here," coaxed Mrs. Smith. Margo dropped the ball between her paws and just sat there, looking happy.

Mrs. Smith said, "We're still working on the part where she brings it back."

Norman decided it wouldn't work out too well to try to teach a plant to sit. But Fluffy was already good at grabbing socks to eat and things to pull himself along with. Maybe he could teach Fluffy to grab on command.

That evening Michael explained to Dad about the seeds being plants now. "Maybe if we offered them triple what they paid," he suggested, "we could get more of them back." At least that had persuaded Chad to think it over.

"And I suppose you want me to put up the cash for this?"

Michael nodded.

"And how many seeds did Jason sell?"

"Maybe sixteen. He's making a list."

"I'm not happy about this," said Dad, "but I guess it would be worth it to avoid all the trouble those plants would cause."

"Thanks!" said Michael. He hurried to call Jason.

Michael told him that they could go up to three dollars for buybacks, with Jason returning the dollar apiece he had sold them for and Dad supplying the other two. Then he wrote down all the names as Jason read from his list.

"Are you sure this is everybody?"

"I think so. There might be one or two more."

"Well, keep trying to remember," said Michael. "I'll talk to you tomorrow about dividing up the names."

There was no school on Friday because of a teachers' conference, so Mom suggested they ask all the kids with plants to bring them to school on Monday. Then she could come with the car to pick the plants up in one trip.

Before Michael went to sleep he looked over the list again. It looked like more than fifteen or sixteen names. He counted them. There were twenty-six.

Chapter 3

The next morning Michael woke up to the sound of Norman saying over and over, "Grab, Fluffy, grab!" With each command, Norman would wind a vine around his wrist and wait to see what Fluffy would do. A few times he felt the vine tighten a little. Most of the time nothing happened. Norman kept trying.

At school that day Jason and Michael got eleven takers for the three dollar offer. Michael checked them off the list. Kimberly Offenberg, Pat Jenkins, and Chad said no. Four others were thinking it over.

After school Brad Chan caught up with Michael on the street and said he would bring his plant back Monday for the three dollars. "Great," said Michael. He took the list from his pocket to check him off. Brad was not on the list.

Two kids brought their tiny plants to school on Thursday because they wanted their three dollars as soon as possible. Michael told them they would have to wait until Monday to get paid.

Now he still had to figure out a way to persuade the holdouts to sell. While his class was doing a math lesson, his mind began to wander. Staring at the multiplication problems on the board, he got a good idea. One of the ways he had persuaded his parents to let him and Norman keep their plants was by showing them it would be cheaper to feed socks to two plants for a year than pet food to a couple of cats or dogs.

He started by multiplying what he remembered a pair of socks usually cost at the Save-A-Lot discount store times three hundred and sixty-five days a year. Then he multiplied by two because at more expensive stores surely socks would cost twice as much and he needed the biggest total he could get. He doubled that number because the plants were eating more some nights. He added on a wild guess at the cost of orange juice for a year. The total looked impressive.

Later he told Jason, "We have to tell the holdouts that it'll cost them about six hundred dollars a year to buy special plant food."

"That much?" asked Jason, looking shocked. "Just for socks?"

Michael replied, "They're eating orange juice now, too. We have to hurry. If we're going to get all the plants back by Monday, we have to tell everybody today."

This got results.

"Are you kidding?" exclaimed Chad. "Why didn't you tell me that before? If I had that kind of money, I'd start saving up for a Lamborghini! Give me my three bucks. I'll bring the plant back Monday."

Kimberly Offenberg said, "I'd have to give up my gymnastics lessons. You can have it back."

Pat Jenkins asked Michael, "Are you sure the real reason you want all these plants back isn't that you don't want anybody else to have ones as good as yours and your brother's for Pet Plant Day?''

"I'm sure," replied Michael.

"Okay," agreed Pat. "I'm going to have another great plant anyway.''

"What kind?" he asked.

"I'm not telling," said Pat. Michael figured she wasn't telling because she didn't know yet, but he was sure she would come up with something unusual.

All the other holdouts also said yes. They were delighted to be making two dollars on the deal.

Michael walked home with the two little plants peeping out of his backpack.

"Just put them in a corner of the dining room," said Mom. "They'll be out of the way there.''

At dinner Michael told Dad he was going to need more money than planned for buybacks. He explained, "Twenty-seven plants times three dollars equals—uh.''

"Eighty-one," said Dad. "And Jason is giving back a dollar apiece, so that leaves fifty-four dollars I have to give you. Has anybody thought about what we're going to do with all these small plants?"

"A compost pile," said Mom. "I'll add my vegetable and fruit peelings, too. When they turn to good dirt, we'll use it to enrich the soil and start a little garden to grow our own salads. Won't it be wonderful just to step out the back door and pick lettuce and tomatoes and herbs for dinner?"

"No," said Norman. "I want to keep all the baby plants.''

"We can't," said Mom firmly. "Picture twenty-seven plants as big as Stanley and Fluffy, which is what they would look like after a while. It would be like living in an indoor jungle. We couldn't move without bumping into them. And what if they started running around the house at night? There'd be a plant traffic jam."

"Not if we feed them enough," Norman pointed out.

"How many thousands of socks and gallons of orange juice would that take? It would cost zillions. We'll start the compost pile Monday."

"We could get a traffic light," suggested Norman. Everybody ignored him.

Dad said, "That pile of garbage is going to cost me fifty-four bucks."

Mom replied, "Think of the money we'll save on lettuce and tomatoes."

An idea suddenly occurred to Michael. "Maybe," he said, "there might be a way we could get the fifty-four dollars back."

"How?" asked Dad.

"We could try to sell the baby plants to Dr. Sparks. We only gave her six seeds. I bet she'd like more plants for her experiments."

"Good thinking," said Dad.

"Okay," said Mom. "Why not? They should be back from their vacation by Monday. I'll call her then. If she doesn't want them, then we'll compost."

After dinner Norman asked, "Can I sleep over at Bob's tonight?"

Mom asked, "This is sort of short notice. Did they invite you?"

"Yes," said Norman. "I just forgot to ask. Can I? Please, please, please?"

"I guess it's all right since there's no school tomorrow," she agreed. "I'll call his mother to tell her okay."

Norman rushed off to pack a duffel bag. He lined everything up on his bed first. Then he packed very neatly—a set of clean clothes for morning, pajamas, robe, slippers, hairbrush, toothbrush, and his rubber gorilla head.

He zipped up the bag and slung the handle over his shoulder. Now he was all set except for one thing.

Mom stopped him at the front door as he was heading out with Fluffy.

"I said you could go. Not Fluffy."

"But Bob invited him, too."

"No, your plant is not allowed to go on sleepovers."

"But," began Norman.

"No buts," said Mom. "That's final."

"Why?" he whined.

"We're not taking a chance on a plant acting up at somebody else's house."

"I want Fluffy to go with me," he complained, pouting.

"One more whine," said Mom, "and you'll get to stay home, too. Go ahead. I'll put Fluffy back in your room."

He started down the front walk. Mom waved and called, "Behave yourself! Don't stay up too late! Don't make too much noise! Don't jump on the beds! Have a good time!"

As she pulled the plant back to make room to close the door, she did not notice Fluffy waving a vine in Norman's direction.

Michael was happy to have the whole room to himself for a change. He was going to stay up late reading and listening to tapes he liked that Norman hated. He opened the closet door and kicked his shoes off so they landed in there.

He pulled off his dirty socks, dropped them in front of Stanley, and got a clean pair out of a drawer for Fluffy. He got a glass of orange juice from the kitchen, smeared some on each plant's vines and leaves, and poured the rest around their roots.

"Now you're all set for the night," he told them.

Without Norman there, he could be as messy as he wanted. Of course, he would have to pick everything up and put it away before he went to bed so the plants couldn't eat anything that might make them sick. Stanley had once gotten horribly ill from a plastic toy car, and Fluffy had been poisoned by accidentally eating a sock with a musical microchip and battery in it.

So for a few joyful minutes Michael acted like his natural messy self. As he took off his clothes, he tossed them into the air, then caught them and tossed them again and let them fall all over. When he tossed his underpants the third time, they went up but did not come down. They got stuck on the ceiling light.

While Michael tried to figure out how to get them down without going out to the garage for a ladder, he put on his pajamas, the ones Grandma had sent him for his birthday. They had pictures of spaceships all over them. Pajamas with pictures were for little kids like Norman, who had turtles all over his favorite pair. But these were the only pajamas Michael could find. His others must be in the wash.

It occurred to him that sleeping in his underwear would be more comfy than these stiff new pajamas. But there was no clean underwear in his underwear drawer. So he would have to sleep in what he just took off, but first he would have to get the bottom half down from the ceiling.

First he took one of Stanley's vines and tried to direct it to the dangling underpants. He explained to his plant what he wanted done, but Stanley refused to move.

Maybe standing on the bed would work. He grabbed the footboard and swung it around so part of the bed was under the light. He climbed up and started bouncing with one arm outstretched.

There was a rap on the door. Dad walked in. "What's going on?" he asked.

"I can't get my underpants off the ceiling," Michael explained. Dad stepped up on the bed and reached them easily.

Mom walked in. "Why are you two standing on the bed?" she asked. They explained.

She said, "If I wrote a book about this family, nobody would believe it."

Dad shoved the bed back where it belonged. Mom scooped up Michael's clothes from all over the room. As she took them away to put in the wash, she said sternly. "Remember our deal. To get to keep the plants, you promised to be neat."

"I was going to pick it all up," Michael said.

Dad asked Michael, "Did you take the trash out yet?"

"I forgot," he replied.

"Get going," said Dad.

"Do I have to? I don't want to get dressed all over again. Besides, all my clothes are in the wash."

"It's your turn," said Dad firmly. "Just put on your shoes and do it. It'll only take a minute, and it's dark out. Nobody will see you."

"I'll do it in the morning," he said.

19

"Now," said Dad. "We don't want to miss the pickup. Those trucks come at the crack of dawn."

"How do you know that?" Michael asked, trying to stall.

"Because," said Dad, "they make so much noise that your mother says they wake her up at the crack of dawn every Friday."

So Michael trudged back and forth from the garage to the curb three times. He lugged out recycling buckets of aluminum, glass, and plastic, the stack of newspapers, and the trash can full of all the other junk.

It was dark out, as Dad said, but the street light near their house shone brightly on Michael's spaceship pajamas.

On the last trip he met Mrs. Smith, out walking her dog. She smiled, said hello, and added, "What a cute outfit!"

Back in his room, Michael kicked his shoes into the closet again and plopped down on his bed to read. He finally fell asleep with the book on his stomach. When Mom looked in on him later, she put the book in a drawer and turned out the light.

Long after the light went out, the plants began stirring as usual and ate their nightly meals. This was followed by hearty burps and Fluffy's "ex," a noise he had been making ever since Norman tried to teach him to say "excuse me."

The plants settled down again. Stanley gently put a vine on Michael's shoulder. Fluffy reached out for Norman. But there was no familiar head on the pillow. Fluffy felt around the whole bed and found nothing. He stood there, vines dangling, for a little while. Then he began pulling himself out of the room.

20

Fluffy slowed dragged himself from room to room looking for Norman. On his travels he yanked on a few things that fell over, but nothing broke. He kept going until he got to the front door. There he pulled on the handle, but it didn't budge. After a few more tries, he managed to wrap his vine around and around the handle enough to turn it.

The door opened. Fluffy let go, reached outside, and found a little outdoor light pole. He yanked on that so hard that he flung himself out of the house with so much force that he rolled down the front walk. Letting go, he rolled on and bumped to a stop over the edge of the grass between the sidewalk and the curb.

There he stood, stuck, right next to the trash.

Chapter 4

Michael woke up early because Stanley pulled the covers off him. He sat up on the edge of his bed. Something was wrong. No Norman. No Fluffy.

Then he remembered that Norman was at Bob's. But where was Fluffy? Probably in the kitchen again.

He padded down the hall to get him. This was getting to be a nuisance.

But Fluffy was not in the kitchen. Michael glanced into the living room and everywhere else, even the bathroom. A few things were knocked over, so Fluffy must have been wandering around. But the plant was gone.

Don't panic, he told himself. There has to be a logical explanation. The last time Fluffy was missing Norman had taken his plant for a walk. Could he have come home late last night and taken Fluffy to Bob's? That didn't seem logical, but with Norman anything was possible. Michael decided he'd better check that first before waking up Mom and Dad.

It was too early to call. That would wake up Bob's whole family. He didn't want to go down the street in his pajamas, and he was in a hurry to go back to bed, so he unlocked the kitchen door and hurried through the backyards.

At Bob's house he looked in the ground floor window he knew was Bob's room. He rapped hard on the glass and called Norman's name. Both boys woke up.

"Is Fluffy with you?" asked Michael.

"He's home," said Norman, looking alarmed.

"No, he's not. I looked all over the house."

"We have to find him!" said Norman.

"I'm coming, too," said Bob.

Two blocks away the recycling truck rounded the corner and stopped. Two men lifted pails of cans and glass and emptied them noisily.

Soon, behind them came a huge trash truck. Another man emptied trash cans into the back of that. With a great grinding crunch, the machinery ground the trash into smithereens.

By the time Michael got around to Bob's front door, Norman and Bob had run out. As they turned onto the sidewalk toward home, Norman spotted Fluffy standing by the curb far down the street.

"There he is!" he yelled and started running. Michael was relieved. He followed at a walk since the crisis was over. Bob was right behind him.

The rattle and crash of glass jars and the clatter of cans being dumped into the bins of the recycling truck woke Mom as usual.

She sat up sleepily and grumbled, "There ought to be a law to make them do that quietly."

Dad replied without opening his eyes, "There's no way to crash glass quietly."

From a distance could be heard the grinding of the trash truck, slowly coming closer.

Since she was awake anyway, Mom decided she might as well get up and enjoy some quiet time before everyone else got up.

She slid her feet around, feeling for her slippers. Instead she found her sneakers right where she'd kicked them off the night before. She wiggled her feet into them, not bothering to tie the laces. She was only going as far as the front door to get the newspaper.

As Norman hurried toward Fluffy he paid no attention to the trash trucks. They were always there early every Friday morning.

Then he saw the recycling truck was pulling up right in front of Fluffy. A man hopped off and started emptying recycling buckets. That didn't worry Norman because Fluffy was not made of glass or aluminum.

He started running a little faster. He thought he'd better get Fluffy back in the house before the noise of the trash trucks woke Mom up. It was going to be close.

He stopped to look both ways before crossing the street and then started running faster to cover the last block.

As the recycling truck pulled away from Fluffy, he saw looming behind it the giant trash truck, rolling slowly, clanking and roaring, toward Fluffy.

The workman following the truck hoisted the garbage can next to the plant and emptied it into the open maw of the truck. Then he tossed the can back on the grass and reached for Fluffy.

Norman, almost there, screamed, "Nooooooo!"

The man looked up, startled to see three boys in pajamas running his way down the sidewalk. The smaller boy in front looked upset. Was he being chased by the others?

The man grabbed the plant with both hands to move it aside so he could step forward to help the running boy. Beside him the truck's compactor was chomping trash into teensy pieces.

Norman knew what that noise meant.

He leaped at the workman, tackled him around the knees, and snarled, "Let go my Fluffy!"

The man nearly fell over from surprise. "Your what?" he replied, clearly baffled. Norman hung on like an attack dog.

The man let go of the plant so he could use his hands to pry Norman loose from his legs.

Michael caught up with them. "Let go of my brother!" he demanded.

"If this is your brother, why were you and that other kid chasing him?"

"We weren't. We were running to save his plant."

The man replied, "This can't be his plant. It was put out for pickup by the people who live in this house. I saw you all coming from way down the street."

Norman said indignantly, "This is too my plant, and this is our house!"

"Oh, sure," said the man. "And your mother lets you run around the neighborhood at dawn in your pajamas. And if this was your plant, why would you put it out for pickup if you didn't want to get rid of it?"

"He must have got out by accident," explained Norman. He grabbed Fluffy and pulled the plant toward him on the sidewalk.

"Very funny," said the man. "I suppose what you really want is the skateboard this big pot is wired to. But it's against the law to take other people's trash.

You'd have to get permission from the people who live here.''

The truck horn honked. ''Come on,'' called the driver. ''We don't want to get behind schedule!''

The man stepped forward to grab the plant.

But Norman was too fast for him. He gave Fluffy a hard shove that started the plant rolling down the sloping sidewalk. He yelled, ''Run, Fluffy, run!''

The truck, headed in the opposite direction, started to move along. The man looked at the departing plant, which was rolling faster and faster as it went downhill. Norman was running after it.

''I give up,'' said the man. ''I guess if he can catch it, he can keep it!'' He turned and followed the truck to the pile of trash in front of the next house. Michael and Bob ran after Norman.

While Mom put coffee and water into the coffee maker, she was wondering why the trash truck sounded like it was standing in front of their house for so long. What were they doing out there?

Just as she went to the front door to get the newspaper, she heard the truck move on. Then she opened the door and was amazed to see first Bob, and beyond him Michael, and ahead of him Norman, all running away. In the distance she saw Fluffy, leading the parade.

When the garbage man turned around to pick up another can next door, he saw a woman in pink pajamas sprint out the front door and follow the boys running after the plant. Her untied purple robe flapped behind her like the cape of a comic book hero.

Maybe those kids really do live there, he thought.

Even the mother runs around the neighborhood in pajamas. Weird, he thought, very weird.

Dad was still asleep when the bedside phone rang. It was Mrs. Smith. "Is anything wrong over there?" she asked. "Do you need any help?"

"Help?" asked Dad foggily.

She explained, "I just saw your wife run out the front door in her pajamas. She was heading south down the sidewalk. That seemed a little unusual, so I thought I'd better check."

The garbage man, now two houses away, looked up again to see a barefooted man in green pajamas run out of the same house. He yanked frantically at the door handle of the car in the drive. Then he ran back indoors, came out with keys, unlocked the car, and zoomed away.

When Dad caught up with Mom, he slowed down and kept honking the horn to get her attention. When she finally realized that it was Dad and not some nut, he pulled over and she jumped in.

"Hurry!" she said. "Fluffy's gotten loose somehow, and the boys are trying to catch him." Then she added, "At least, I think that's what's happening."

Far ahead, Norman was running easily because the sidewalk slanted gently downhill. But he could not run as fast as Fluffy could roll. On the slope, Fluffy was gaining speed.

"Fluffy!" yelled Norman. "Wait up!"

But the plant seemed to be enjoying running free. His leaves flapped in the breeze created by going faster and faster. His vines trailed behind him like some kind of funny-looking long hair.

"Oh, no!" yelled Norman. His plant was racing toward a street! "Look out!" he called.

Chapter 5

Fluffy did not stop to look both ways. Norman watched in horror as the plant zoomed off the curb, airborne. Fortunately, there were no cars coming. Fluffy hit the street with a thump that almost tipped him over. He wobbled and swayed to one side and then the other. Norman hoped he would bump to a stop against the opposite curb. But the skateboard caromed off the curb, sending Fluffy rolling, a bit slower now, along in the street.

When Norman got to the corner, he stopped to look both ways and then sprinted across and up onto the sidewalk.

By now Dad and Mom had picked up Bob and were closing in on Michael.

"What exactly is going on here?" Mom asked Bob.

"Michael pounded on my window and wanted to know where Fluffy was," explained Bob. "Then the trash man attacked Fluffy, and Norman attacked the trash man right back. It was great!"

Dad asked Mom, "Is this starting to make sense?"

"Not yet," she replied.

Michael jumped into the car and said, "This isn't my fault. I didn't start this." They had almost caught up to Norman.

Honking the horn and calling Norman's name, they slowed down, but Norman kept running.

"Get in the car!" commanded Mom.

"No, I have to save Fluffy!" he yelled back. They drove along beside him.

Michael suggested from the back seat, "Could we cut Fluffy off if we speed up and drive around in front of him?"

"It's worth a try," said Dad, passing Norman. "But Fluffy is going to bang into the car."

"It's better than letting him get run over by a truck or smithereened by crashing into a building," Michael said.

"True," agreed Dad. "The farther he goes, the faster he goes, and the harder he's going to hit. And this street goes downhill only a couple of more blocks. Then it ends at the river."

"Oh, no!" said Bob. "We can't let Fluffy drown!"

"It's now or never," said Dad.

They were catching up to Fluffy. Just ahead the plant sailed through another intersection. As the car neared the intersection a huge trash truck suddenly pulled out in front of them. Dad slammed on the brakes. The car screeched to a standstill a few feet from the truck.

As they waited for the truck to move slowly out of the way, Norman caught up with the car. But he didn't get in. He stopped at the curb to look both ways, carefully went around the back of the truck, and then ran on as fast as he could.

In the street potholes here and there were slowing Fluffy down a little but not enough.

In the distance Norman saw the wide muddy river.

He remembered how the steep banks plunged down to the water. If the low guardrail did not lop Fluffy in half, it would flip him right over into the deep water.

Norman stopped and mustered up all his lung power, which was considerable. He took a deep breath and yelled, "Grab, Fluffy, grab! Grab anything!"

Nobody could ever be sure exactly what caused Fluffy to do what he did, but Norman was convinced that Fluffy heard him.

His plant suddenly flung its vines forward and to both sides, whirling them like lariats in all directions. One vine snaked around a telephone pole, but it started to slip away. Norman was running again, yelling "Grab! Grab! You can do it!"

Another vine hit the telephone pole and wrapped around, then another. They all held, stopping Fluffy with such a hard jerk that the plant was yanked up over the curb and whirled around the pole until it slowed to a safe stop.

Norman ran up and hugged Fluffy and the pole.

The few people passing at that early hour were treated to the sight of four people in pajamas piling out of a car. The two big ones ran over to hug a small boy, also in pajamas, who was hugging a large weird plant, whose vines were hugging a telephone pole.

Dad and Mom were so glad that nothing terrible had happened to Norman during his frantic run that they forgot to get mad at him.

Dad pried Norman loose from Fluffy. "It's okay," he reassured him, "we'll take him home now." To get Fluffy loose from the pole, Norman started pushing the plant around it to unwind the vines.

"Well, he won't fit in the car," said Mom. "He'll have to be rolled home."

"Uphill all the way," said Michael. "Ugh."

"In our pajamas," pointed out Bob.

"We'll take turns pushing," said Dad, "two at a time."

There was more traffic on the streets now. People were slowing up in their cars to stare at this unusual group.

Dad said, "The sooner we get started, the sooner it'll be over." He tossed Mom the car keys. "Go home and get us some clothes to put on over these pajamas."

"I'll call Bob's house," she said, "to let them know where he is. They must be worried sick by now."

She drove away. Dad and Norman started pushing Fluffy homeward. Michael, following with Bob, felt like an idiot out for a stroll in his pajamas. He wished Mom would hurry up.

Back home Mom dashed in the front door and ran smack into something she hadn't expected to be there— Bob's mother.

"Do you know where the boys are?" asked Bob's mother frantically.

"They're fine," said Mom. "We found them. They're on the way home."

"Thank goodness," said Bob's mother. "What happened? I woke up and they were gone! So I called here and there was no answer. Then I drove over and the front door was unlocked."

Mom told her about the plant chase, although she wasn't quite sure how it had all started.

While Mom gathered up clothes, Bob's mother called her husband to tell him the good news. And she added, "Call the police back and tell them to stop looking."

* * *

But a policeman had already found them. Dad was explaining that he had not kidnapped Norman and Bob from Bob's house. Then he explained why they were out for a walk in their pajamas along with a very large plant.

From the look on the policeman's face Michael could tell that the officer thought they were a bunch of wackos but probably harmless wackos.

The officer said he would stop at their house to double-check their story. "You have to admit this looks a bit strange," he said.

"You're right about that," agreed Dad.

Soon afterward Mom pulled up in the car, followed by Bob's mother in her car. She told Bob, "Don't you ever leave the house again without telling us!" Bob waved goodbye as they drove away.

Mom handed over shirts and pants for her family to put on over their pajamas to look semi-normal. A few drivers slowed to get a better look at what appeared to be three people getting dressed on a street corner.

Mom joked, "I'm sorry I couldn't find something for Fluffy to wear, but nothing would fit."

"It's easy for you to make wisecracks," grumbled Dad. "You're not the one stuck pushing this thing home."

Mom tried to console him. "You're almost halfway there," she pointed out, "and you don't look nearly so funny now that you've got clothes on over your pajamas."

"Thanks a lot!" said Dad. "Come on, guys, push!"

"I'll have breakfast ready when you get home," called Mom.

Back at the house she found a police car in the driveway. Mrs. Smith and some other neighbors had come over to find out what was going on. They stayed to hear Mom explain what had happened and backed up her story that hers was a law-abiding family.

During breakfast Norman parked Fluffy in the kitchen because he did not want to let him out of his sight.

Dad announced, ''We have to do something drastic. We can't have Fluffy running away from home like this.''

Mom said, ''He needs to be locked up somewhere that he can't escape from. Too bad there isn't a zoo for wild plants.''

Norman wailed, ''But he would never run away from home!''

''Then why on earth did he go out of the house?'' asked Mom. ''The time when both plants came to the kitchen they were looking for juice.'' She turned to Michael. ''Didn't you feed them both the usual socks and juice last night?''

''Of course I did,'' he replied.

''Then,'' said Mom, ''Fluffy wasn't hungry and looking for food.''

Norman protested, ''He must have got out by accident!''

Michael was puzzled by this mystery. ''Maybe something set him off,'' he suggested.

''Like what?'' asked Dad.

''I was jumping on my bed last night. Maybe that upset him. But no, Norman does that all the time. It never bothered Fluffy before.'' He tried to picture the room last night and ran over in his mind everything that happened before he fell asleep. Then he realized what was wrong with that picture.

''Aha!'' exclaimed Michael. ''The only thing really

different about the room last night was that Norman's bed didn't have Norman in it.''

"So?'' asked Mom.

Michael explained, "Ever since Fluffy was a seed, he's never been away from Norman at night—even when we went on vacation—except for a few nights at Grandma's because she wouldn't let us bring the plants in the house. Then they were locked up in the RV. So the logical explanation is that Fluffy was not escaping or running away. He was looking for Norman.''

"Oh, Fluffy!'' exclaimed Norman, sniffling. He flung his arms around the plant. Fluffy gathered all his vines around Norman, who almost disappeared into the greenery.

Watching this, Michael felt a little choked up, too.

Mom said to Dad, "That explanation makes sense, sort of, doesn't it?''

"I guess so,'' said Dad. He put his arm around Mom. "Now all we have to do to keep Fluffy from escaping is to make sure Norman never goes anywhere overnight again.''

"Oh, no,'' said Mom. "That means all the sleepovers he ever wants to go on will have to be at our house.''

Chapter 6

The weekend was quiet except for Norman practicing grab commands with Fluffy early every morning. When he tired of that, he put his plant at one end of the hall and rolled an old tennis ball at him from the other end. After hundreds of tries, Fluffy finally flicked a vine at the ball, knocking it back to Norman.

"Good plant!" said Norman in the same tone of voice that Mrs. Smith used to tell Margo "Good dog!" He rousted Michael out of bed to show him Fluffy's latest accomplishment.

"That's great," said Michael sincerely. But he also felt jealous that he hadn't thought of teaching something like that to Stanley. He wished he could think of something better.

News of the plant buybacks had spread all over school, so the principal, Mr. Leedy, was not surprised to see twenty-five kids carrying plants into the office Monday morning. The school secretary found herself surrounded by flower pots of all sizes and colors. Other kids, who had seen Stanley and Fluffy when they were already very large at the science fair, gathered to see what the little ones looked like.

They were many sizes, ranging from a green dot just coming out of the dirt to six inches high.

"What are you going to do with these?" everyone kept asking.

Michael told them, "We know a scientist who's trying to find out what kind they are. She's already doing botany research with some seeds we gave her."

Mom brought some cardboard boxes along to put them in for easier carrying.

Back home, she put the boxes on the floor in the dining room.

She called Susan Sparks at work.

"I'm glad you called," said Dr. Sparks. "I was going to call you this week about getting some more seeds. But we just got back last night, and I'm trying to catch up here."

Mom told her about the twenty-seven plants.

Dr. Sparks said, "I'd be happy to buy them. Could you come for a weekend as soon as possible? We're only about a five-hour drive from there, and you can stay with us. We'd love to have you, and Max and Sarah would enjoy having Norman and Michael visit."

"Maybe we could come right after school's out," said Mom.

"If you can make it sooner, please do," said Dr. Sparks. "I'm eager to try to train plants to pick things up like Stanley and Fluffy. And I have a lot more questions to ask the boys."

In Florida they'd finally told Dr. Sparks that their plants ate socks in the middle of the night, but luckily she hadn't believed them. She thought they'd dreamed it or were kidding. The night she sat up to watch their plants, the boys made sure Stanley and Fluffy would not eat any socks, so she'd only seen the plants picking up and dropping socks.

Mom agreed to send more seeds right away and to bring the little plants when they visited. She asked, "Have you figured out yet what kind of plants these are?"

"No," replied Dr. Sparks. "I told some of my co-workers about them this morning, but they didn't know offhand. I'll check with some more experts. Wouldn't it be wonderful if these turn out to be a new species?"

"Is that possible?" asked Mom.

"Oh, yes," said Dr. Sparks. "Unknown ones are discovered all the time, especially in rain forests."

"That's amazing," said Mom.

Dr. Sparks said, "Plant life is always amazing. That's one of the reasons I love being a botanist. Oh, one other thing. Be sure not to let anything happen to any of your plants or seeds. As far as we know, except for the six seeds you gave us, the ones you have may be the only other ones there are."

Mom said, "Like an endangered species?"

"Could be," said Dr. Sparks. "We don't want to take any chances."

When Mom told the whole family what Dr. Sparks said, she explained, "So we're stuck with the little plants until we go to the Sparkses. But until then, I don't want them getting any bigger than absolutely necessary. No feeding them anything extra. Just enough water to keep them going. And don't let them get anywhere near a sock." The boys promised.

Dad asked Mom, "Have you talked to your mother about her plant yet?"

Mom got the same look on her face that Michael always got when he had put off something he didn't want to do. "I've been meaning to," she said. There was a long pause. "Okay, I'll do it right now. Unfortunately, after what Susan said about endangered species, my weed killer idea is out."

Michael said, "But Grandma said she's growing it in her bathroom. If we just tell her not to leave any socks in there, then there won't be any problem. And her plant is on the sink, not a skateboard, so it can't go anywhere."

Mom asked, "Do you want to explain to her why she shouldn't leave her own socks in her own bathroom?"

Michael grinned. "You can explain it to her better," he said.

"You're going to tell her about the sock-eating?" inquired Norman. He looked puzzled because Mom and Dad had made him and Michael promise not to tell.

"I guess I have to," said Mom. "You know how she enjoys growing interesting plants. She won't want to part with it unless she knows she's harboring a monster. Maybe I can get her to send it to us by an overnight delivery service since it's still small enough to fit in a box." She headed for the phone.

The boys and Dad stayed very quiet so they could hear her talking in the kitchen.

"The real reason we need to get it back," she was explaining, "is that this kind of plant causes big problems. The vines are—uh—very active at night. You wouldn't want to keep one of these in your house.

"How active? Well, they eat socks and pull themselves along on their skateboards. Norman's even escaped from the house.

"No, I am not joking. This is serious. Yes, we're

39

letting the boys keep theirs, but— No, I haven't actually seen them eat socks. They do it when we're asleep. But the boys have seen them doing it. And the socks are always gone in the morning. But I myself have personally seen them move themselves around.

"Yes, really. I know it sounds nuts, but it's true. But—oh, mother, no, you don't want to do that! Hmmm. Well, okay, I'll talk to you next weekend."

Mom came back in the living room.

"What did she say?" asked Michael.

"She's keeping it," replied Mom. "She doesn't really believe it will do anything, but if it does, she thinks that would be really interesting. And, just to see what happens, when it gets a little bigger, she's going to buy it a skateboard!"

Chapter 7

The seedlings grew slowly. By the end of another week, some were peeping over the tops of the boxes. Many were starting to develop little vines.

"Why are some of them bigger?" wondered Norman.

Michael replied, "Everybody must have used different dirt. Some dirt is more nutritious for plants."

Norman screwed up his face and said, "Ooo, ugh!" at the thought.

"And delicious," added Michael with a chuckle, just to make Norman squirm.

In another week, while the family slept and Stanley and Fluffy ate socks, the little plants in the dining room were waving tiny vines and trying to feel around.

Two of the bigger ones in separate boxes next to each other reached out and got tangled up. Trying to get untangled, they started having a tug-of-war.

Next morning Mom found the loser pulled out of its pot and lying between the boxes, still tangled with the winner. Dirt was scattered around its roots.

"What's going on here?" she said loudly. The boys and Dad came in from the kitchen to see. Michael put the plant back in its pot, and Norman started cleaning up the dirt.

"I wonder what happened," said Michael. "Stanley and Fluffy never pulled each other out of their pots."

Norman replied, "These must have been arm wrestling."

They took all the plants out of the boxes and spaced them far enough apart around the room so they couldn't reach each other. All of them wouldn't fit that way in the dining room, so the boys put a few in the living room and a couple in the hall. Mom refused to let them use twenty-seven of her dishes to put under the pots so water wouldn't leak out the holes in the bottoms and ruin the rugs. She made them use big pieces of plastic.

Dad said, "This will prevent any chance of more plant wrestling."

"Terrific," said Mom. "Now it looks like plants are oozing all over the house!"

Michael added, "This will keep them out of trouble until we take them to Dr. Sparks." Mom still looked irritated.

Dad told her, "Just be glad these little ones aren't on skateboards."

The boys counted out twenty seeds from each of the big plants to send to Dr. Sparks. They labeled the plastic bags "Fluffy Seeds" and "Stanley Seeds." There were still plenty left in the two pails of pods in their closet.

A few days later a package arrived from Dr. Sparks. In it was a huge book about plants full of color pictures. In the letter with it, she thanked the family for the seeds and said she had planted all forty of them.

42

Norman commented, "She must have a bigger dining room than we do!"

Michael said, "She probably planted them where she works."

The letter also said that although she had mentioned in Florida that she was going to send them each a book, she was sending this big one for them to share. Inside the book she had written:

To Michael and Norman
I thought you might enjoy reading about some other plants that do amazing things.
Happy growing,
             Your botanist friend, Susan Sparks

The boys immediately got into a squabble about who would get to read the book first. Michael grabbed it and announced, "Me first because it says 'To Michael and Norman,' not 'To Norman and Michael.' "

This book was much thicker and heavier than the ones Michael usually read. He sat on the couch and started leafing through, looking at the pictures and stopping to read interesting parts before going back to start at page one.

Norman popped up behind him and hung over the back of the couch, reading over his shoulder. Michael ignored him.

"Don't turn that page yet," complained Norman. "I'm not through!"

"Get away from me," snarled Michael. "You're driving me crazy."

"Good," said Norman.

Michael got up, pushed a chair up against the wall

with no room behind it for Norman, and sat down in it. Norman hung over the arm.

"Stop it!" protested Michael. "You're making a big shadow on the page!"

"Am not!"

"Are too!" said Michael. But then he got so interested in what was on the page that he forgot about being pestered.

"This is amazing!" he said. "The voodoo plant, also called the devil's tongue, blooms only one week a year with a flower that stinks so bad that nobody wants to go near it."

"Pew," said Norman. "I wonder why Stanley doesn't stink after he eats so many of your smelly dirty socks."

Michael swatted him with a small nearby pillow and babbled on enthusiastically. "This voodoo plant smells like rotten meat, and that attracts bugs that love rotten meat. Then when they get there and there isn't any, they get the flower's pollen on them and spread it around."

Norman said, "I bet the bugs get mad when they find out they were faked out."

A few pages further, Michael said, "Did you know that morning glories open up before dawn and close about noon? And moonflowers and evening primroses open their flowers at night. And these are called four o'clocks because they stay closed all day and open up about four in the afternoon. Amazing!"

Norman said, "You could put one on your arm so you'd always know when it's four o'clock if you don't have a watch."

"You can't plant a flower on your arm," said Michael scornfully.

"What about daylight saving time?" asked Norman.

"What about it?"

"Then do four o'clocks still open at four o'clock? Or

at three o'clock or five o'clock? What time is four o'clock in daylight saving time?''

Michael replied, ''Four o'clock.''

''No, I mean what time is it really?''

''I don't know and don't care,'' said Michael. ''Go ask Mom.''

Norman found her at the dining room table, surrounded by plants on the floor. She was writing checks and adding up bills on her calculator.

He asked, ''Do four o'clock flowers open up at four o'clock or three o'clock or five o'clock when it's daylight saving time?''

''Well, let's see,'' said Mom. ''I always have to stop and think about that. The saying is, 'Spring forward, fall back.' That means turn the clock forward one hour in the spring when daylight saving time starts and back one hour when it ends in the fall.''

''Huh?'' said Norman, looking confused.

She continued, ''So in spring four o'clock becomes five. And the flowers would go on opening at the same time.''

''Four,'' said Norman.

''No, five. Five o'clock by the clock is really four o'clock by the sun. The flowers go by the sun, not clocks.''

''Then four o'clock is five o'clock,'' he said.

''No, five is really four, and four is actually three.''

''I don't get it,'' said Norman.

Mom replied, ''After discussing it with you, I don't get it either. Tell you what. Let's plant a few four o'clocks in the backyard this summer. Then you can sit out there with a clock and see what time they open.''

Norman said, ''Why don't four o'clocks change their name to five o'clocks or three o'clocks at daylight saving time?''

Mom said, ''Ask your father.''

45

Chapter 8

Mom kept complaining that the little plants were driving her bats. "I can hardly wait to hand them over to Susan," she said. "Every time I walk around in the dining room with a skirt on, they tickle my ankles and shins."

Norman said, "If it's in the daytime, they're not doing it on purpose."

Dad said, "So just don't walk around in there unless you're wearing jeans. Or taller socks. Besides, you won't have to put up with them much longer, only a couple of weeks."

But Mom was on a complaining roll. "And every time I run the vacuum cleaner," she ranted on, "I have to pick up and put back twenty-seven plants and twenty-seven pieces of plastic."

"Then don't run the vacuum for a couple of weeks," suggested Dad.

Mom answered, "We'd be up to our earlobes in crud." Then she smiled. "Of course, there's no reason why I have to do all the vacuuming myself."

"Oh, no," said Dad.

"Oh, yes," said Mom.

"Okay," agreed Dad. "We'll take turns. Tomorrow Norman. He likes to clean up. The next day Michael. The day after that, me."

Michael groaned. Thinking about the horrible prospect of having to do all that cleanup work gave him an idea of how to get out of it. "Let's call Dr. Sparks," he suggested, "and ask if we could take the plants there this weekend. Tomorrow's Friday."

"Brilliant," said Mom. "If it's not convenient for the Sparkses, we could just go drop off the plants, stay in a motel, and come right back the next morning."

Dad said, "I have to work Saturday morning because we're swamped at the office, so I'll stay home and take care of Norman and the plants."

Great, thought Michael. A trip without Norman whining, singing, counting trucks, and reading all the road signs out loud.

"But I'm going, too," said Norman indignantly.

"No," said Dad. "Remember what happened the last time you went away overnight? We don't want Fluffy getting upset and trying to get out again."

"I want to go," squalled Norman. He clenched his fists and stamped his feet. This hardly ever worked with Mom and Dad, but he was so upset at being left out that anger took him over.

After his outburst, he calmed down and switched to his pathetic look. "I really want to see Dr. Sparks's experiments," he said in a sad little voice. "I want to see Max. He's my friend." He sighed. His lower lip looked as if it would start to tremble any minute now.

Mom pointed out gently, "But if your bed is empty, Fluffy would be very, very lonely."

Norman's eyes lit up. "But he won't be lonely if

47

Dad sleeps in my bed," he said with his most winning smile. "Will he, Dad?" He gave his father a big hug. Dad gave up.

Mom called Dr. Sparks, who said, "This weekend will be fine" and gave her directions.

Late Friday afternoon they got ready to go. Norman gave Dad long, boring instructions about how to lay Fluffy's clean socks meal on the floor in just the right spot. He selected two flavors of socks—pink for strawberry on Friday night and white with brown stripes for fudge ripple Saturday. He also wanted Dad to sing to his plant. Dad didn't go for that idea. Norman offered to tape record some of his singing to play for Fluffy. Dad said no thanks.

Michael changed socks and gave the ones he had worn all day to Dad for Stanley's supper that night. But he had no dirty socks for Saturday. He asked Dad, "Could you feed him one of yours along with one of mine both nights and some extra orange juice? That way if he doesn't like your socks, he won't get too hungry."

They loaded their bags into the car trunk and crammed the little plants into the back seat. Norman beat Michael to the front seat.

"Move over," said Michael.

"No," said Mom. "There are only two seat belts in front, so one of you has to sit in back."

"Not me," said Michael. "Norman should do it. He's smaller." Norman gave him a dirty look.

"You can take turns," said Mom. "We'll stop a few times so you can switch places."

Michael gave up and squeezed into the back seat.

Dad stuck his head in the car window to kiss Mom goodbye. "Drive carefully," he said.

Off they went with Michael scrunched among the little plants. The tallest ones next to him were tickling his elbows.

It was getting late and Michael was on his second turn in the front seat when Mom turned off the highway near brightly lit gas stations and motels.

"Are we there?" asked Norman.

"No, there's something wrong with the car." She pulled into a gas station. The boys got out to stretch while she and an attendant looked under the hood. The problem turned out to be a leaking radiator hose. That could be easily replaced, but not until a mechanic came to work in the morning.

They walked across a parking lot to a huge motel and signed up for a room. Then they carried their bags and the plants to their room.

Mom called the Sparkses to let them know they would be arriving the next morning instead. Then she called Dad to let him know where they were. The call woke him. He had fallen asleep on the couch while watching TV because there was nobody home to talk to. Norman got on the phone to make sure he had fed Fluffy.

"I'm going to do it right now," said Dad. After he hung up, he put out the plants' sock suppers and gave them their orange juice.

At the motel two double beds took up most of the room. The boys placed the plants as far apart as possible all over the floor. Norman arranged them so there was an open path to the bathroom, but they still had to step carefully.

Mom was too tired to make a fuss about this. She crawled into her bed and remarked, "Thank goodness we're getting rid of these tomorrow!"

Michael lay on his side near the edge of the other bed, as far from Norman's feet as possible. The bathroom door was ajar to let some light in. He could see the tops of the plants surrounding the bed. He felt like a giant in the middle of a short forest.

Long after Mom and the boys fell asleep, many of the small plants began stretching their tiny vines. One reached too far, lost its balance, and toppled over behind a chair. Some waved their vines around as if they were dancing to a song only they could hear. It looked a lot like the Hokeypokey.

It took Dad longer than usual to fall asleep in Norman's bed because it felt so different from his own. But at last he drifted off. Except for his quiet breathing, the room was silent for a long time. Then the plants began eating socks with their usual "schlurrrps," followed by burps and Fluffy's "ex."

Fluffy reached out a vine as usual and felt across the pillow until he touched Dad. The vine felt all over Dad's face. His nose twitched, but he did not wake up. The vine paused for a moment. Then it touched Dad's shoulder and relaxed. All was still again.

Just before dawn Dad awoke feeling cramped in the narrow bed. The sky was beginning to get light. The night was almost over, and the plants stood motionless in their regular places. He got up carefully so he wouldn't disturb Fluffy's vine on the pillow, took his

50

alarm clock, and padded across the hall to his and Mom's room. He spread out comfortably in their king-sized bed and soon was fast asleep again.

When the alarm went off, Dad was very surprised to find a vine on his shoulder. Towering next to his bed was Fluffy, keeping him company.

Chapter 9

The car was fixed by nine o'clock. Mom and the boys loaded the plants and set off.

When they finally turned into the Sparkses' drive, Max, who was a year younger than Norman, came running out. "They're here! They're here!" he shouted. Norman hopped out and they started walking like penguins around the yard and laughing. This had been one of their favorite things to do when both families stayed at the same campground in Florida. Max thought anything Norman did was wonderful.

"Did you bring your Blaster?" Max asked.

"I left it at home for my Dad to water Fluffy," he replied. Max looked disappointed. "But I brought my gorilla head," he added. Max smiled.

His sister Sarah, who was Michael's age, came out and peered into the back seat to inspect the plants.

"Some are bigger," she observed.

Michael said casually, "They were planted in different kinds of dirt."

Sarah said, "And probably at different times, too."

"Yeah," said Michael. Why hadn't he thought of that? Sarah certainly did know a lot about plants. She had told him in Florida that she wanted to be a botanist like her mother.

Mr. Sparks came out to greet them and take their bags in. He said, "Susan had to go over to the greenhouse. Sarah can ride along and show you how to get there."

"Me, too, me, too!" insisted Max.

"There's not enough room," said his father.

Mom said, "If we put some plants in the front seat, maybe we can cram everybody in."

Norman and Michael burrowed in among the plants in the back seat and passed enough of them forward to make room for Max. Sarah surrounded herself in the front seat with plants on the floor and on both sides of her and held the rest on her lap.

"It's not far," said Mr. Sparks, waving as they pulled out.

"Thank goodness for that," said Mom.

On the way Michael mentioned, "My class went on a field trip to a greenhouse a couple of years ago. We saw a lot of flowers and tomato plants."

Sarah said, "I bet you never saw a greenhouse like this one." She was right. They drove up to what looked like acres of greenhouses, plus some other buildings, and big fields full of growing things.

"What is this place?" asked Michael. "Some kind of farm?"

Sarah replied, "It's the state university agricultural research center."

Sarah and Max led them into the front building, where they asked the man at the reception desk where their mother was. "I think she's in 16W," he replied. "Do you want me to page her?"

"We can find her," said Sarah. She turned to explain

to the others, "That means the sixteenth greenhouse on the west side."

They came to a tray of liquid on the floor. Sarah and Max walked right through it, getting the soles of their shoes wet.

"Come on," said Sarah. "It's disinfectant, like what you walk through at a swimming pool. It's to make sure we don't track in any germs or bugs that could harm the plants."

She led the way through one greenhouse after another. At the end of each one was a door leading into the next one. Michael noticed the differences in temperature. Some were very warm, others almost chilly. The sun shone through the glass roofs. They passed batch after batch of plants of many kinds and sizes.

Norman asked Max, "Do you ever get lost in here?"

"Not lately," he replied.

On they went through more greenhouses. Sarah said, "Hardly anybody's here because it's Saturday." She opened the next door and yelled, "Mother, we're here!"

At the far end of the building a tall, bushy plant waggled its branches and said, "Welcome earthlings! I'm so glad you've come!" The voice belonged to Dr. Sparks.

Sarah rolled her eyes and said, "Oh, Mother!"

Max said, "She's always doing stuff like that."

The botanist came out from behind the greenery to welcome them. She was wearing a short white lab coat with her jeans and T-shirt, blue knee-high rubber boots, and a green baseball cap that said on the front "Planet of the Plants."

Max said proudly, "We got her that hat for her birthday. We had it made special."

54

Even though Michael thought they had seen enough greenhouses, Dr. Sparks took them on a tour. He was amazed at the computer controlled watering system. Each group of plants got exactly the amount needed at the right times. The computer also transmitted programmed instructions to mix exact recipes of nutrients into the water for feeding the different plants.

Dr. Sparks explained, "We keep most areas hospital clean to prevent any diseases."

Norman asked, "Do plants get sick like with chicken pox?"

"Not people diseases," she replied, "but there are bacteria and viruses and insects that make plants sick."

She showed them little flat round transparent covered dishes with tissue cultures growing in them—tiny plants started from specks of stem placed on a special gelatin. Dr. Sparks said, "We can produce up to one hundred new plants just from one stem."

Mom pointed out, "This is not something you can try at home. Thank goodness."

After they peeked into a couple of laboratories, where nothing was going on because it was Saturday, they came to another door. Dr. Sparks said, "The seeds you sent me are planted in here." When she opened the door, they walked into darkness. She turned on a small dim light.

"Why is it dark in here?" asked Mom. "Why aren't they in a greenhouse?"

Dr. Sparks explained, "Since your plants are only active at night, I'm switching the light cycle for these so it will be easier to study them. We keep them in the dark during the day and turn full light on them at night."

Michael asked, "Is that supposed to fool them into acting like it's night in the daytime?"

"Correct," said Dr. Sparks. "That way we won't have to pay assistants extra to work nights to observe them. During the day we can check on them easily. When they get a few inches high, we'll have student assistants chart what happens and videotape their behaviors. If they turn out to be active just for short periods, then we can reduce the observation times."

Norman looked over the planting trays. He asked, "Did you get my Fluffy seeds all mixed in with the Stanley seeds?"

"No," she replied. "All our plants are labeled. So even if the trays got mixed up, we'd still know which plant every seed came from. That way we can keep accurate records of inherited characteristics from each plant that may be different."

Norman looked baffled. Michael whispered to him, "Like eating dirty socks or clean ones."

"Oh," said Norman aloud. "That means Fluffy seeds will grow up to be like Fluffy, and Stanley seeds will be like Stanley."

Dr. Sparks smiled. "Yes, but some may turn out not exactly the same. Then we select the ones that are different in certain ways and grow more of those. For example, if some are better at picking things up, or are stronger and can pick up heavier things, then we might select those to grow more of."

Mom asked, "Are you still thinking about trying to use plants to pick up litter?"

"I know it's a wild idea," said Dr. Sparks, "but wouldn't it be wonderful if that turned out to be possible? I can just picture them keeping parks and playgrounds clean all over the world!"

Norman said, "People should pick up their own junk. Then they wouldn't have to make plants do all the

56

work." Michael wondered if this remark had been aimed at him, but Norman looked sincerely concerned about plants getting stuck with cleaning up the world.

Sarah said, "Plants already clean the air for us."

Michael laughed. "That's a big enough job," he said.

"First," said Dr. Sparks, "we have to find out if the ones grown under scientific conditions will pick up anything."

They all went out to get the plants out of the car. Dr. Sparks let the children help put the plants in new pots and label them with numbers and S's to show they were from Stanley seeds.

"We'll put these in a separate area," she said. They had to be kept apart for a while, she explained, to make sure they had no insects or diseases.

Norman warned, "You better keep them all far apart. If you don't, they might arm wrestle at night."

Max said, "I want to see that! Mom, can we come back tonight and watch them?"

"Not tonight," said Dr. Sparks, smiling. On their way out to the car, she remarked to Mom, "Your kids have such creative imaginations. I know this is a silly question, but those plants don't actually arm wrestle, do they?"

"A couple of them might have," said Mom. "One morning we found one apparently pulled out of its pot by another one. They were still tangled up."

Dr. Sparks did not laugh. "Did it ever happen again?" she asked.

"No, after that we kept them all far apart, except when we put them in the car, but that was okay because it was during the day."

Norman asked, "Where are the Fluffy pods we gave you in Florida? We didn't see them yet."

Sarah replied, "We started them in the RV before we got back from vacation. They're in our greenhouse at home."

Michael was really impressed. "You have your own greenhouse?" he said.

"Just a small one," said Dr. Sparks. "Sarah's been measuring the seedlings' growth and keeping records on them."

Max told Norman, "One's mine. I named it Baby Fluffy."

In the Sparkses' greenhouse at the back of their house, Norman was delighted to see the six small plants among all the other things growing there.

"They look just like Fluffy," he said, "only smaller."

Mom said, "They look like all the other ones."

"No, they don't," said Norman indignantly. "I can tell the difference."

Max pointed proudly to Baby Fluffy. He said, "My sister named the other ones One, Two, Three, Four, Five."

Sarah showed Michael the charts she was keeping on a clipboard. They were day-by-day lists of how much each plant had grown, any changes, when it was watered, and what nutrients it was fed.

Saturday afternoon the Sparks family took their visitors to the local natural history museum. They saw brilliantly colored gems and minerals, stuffed birds from all over the world, an exhibit about rocks, and the best part—the Hall of Dinosaurs.

Michael, who had read almost every dinosaur book in his school and the public libraries, started showing off by casually mentioning dinosaur facts before they got close enough to read the exhibit signs.

Sarah said, "You know a lot about dinosaurs." She looked impressed.

Towering above them in the center of the lofty room was the black skeleton of an allosaurus, reared up on its huge hind legs and claw toes. The spiky bones of its fifteen-foot tail tapered to a tiny bone at the end. Michael peered up at the monstrous skull and sharp teeth. The short front legs each had three curved twelve-inch claws, which looked ready to grab and rip.

The sign said this creature was from the Upper Jurassic period, one hundred thirty-five million years ago, and had been found in Utah. Michael decided that if time travel ever was actually invented, he would be sure not to set his time machine for Utah back a hundred and thirty-five million years. He loved reading about dinosaurs, but he wouldn't want to meet one of these in person, unless maybe he could time travel in an Army tank.

Nearby, an even bigger skeleton stood on all four of its gigantic legs. Its very long neck and small skull stuck straight out over the onlookers below. Norman and Max were reading the sign and trying to pronounce its name, haplocanthosaurus. They were taking turns getting it wrong.

Sarah pointed out some plant fossils in a glass case. They were impressions in stone of bark, stems, ferns, and leaves.

"Look at these crinoids," she said. "They grew underwater and they're called sea lillies, but it says here they were really animals, even though they look like plants."

Michael thought the tops looked exactly like the big

tassels on his grandmother's dining room drapes, but he didn't say so.

On the way out of the hall they saw a slab of dark rock with what looked like giant bird tracks in it.

"Dinosaur tracks," announced Michael. "That rock used to be mud when they ran across it."

In the gift shop Mr. Sparks treated all the kids to small fossils.

Sarah got a little piece of rock with a leaf shape in it. Michael picked out a trilobite, and Max and Norman chose fossilized shark teeth.

Michael said, "I didn't know you could buy fossils. I thought they were all in museums."

"No," said Sarah. "There are so many of some kinds that you can buy them cheap."

All the way back to the Sparkses' house in their van, Michael held his fossil in his hand and kept looking at it. He could hardly believe that he was holding something eons old, that had actually lived when dinosaurs walked the earth.

That night after dinner, they relaxed in front of the fireplace. Dr. Sparks got out a notebook and a tape recorder.

"Now for my research, I need to know a complete history of your plants, everything from the time you got the seeds in the mail until now."

"What exactly do you mean by everything?" asked Michael.

Mom said, "Go ahead. Don't leave anything out. I think she really needs to know the whole truth."

"Truth?" said Dr. Sparks. "What exactly do you mean by that?"

Norman piped up, "They eat socks every night. You

didn't believe us when we told you that in Florida, but it's true. I thought maybe it was raccoons, but it was really Stanley. Then Fluffy did it, too."

Dr. Sparks, Mr. Sparks, and Sarah looked dumbfounded. Max didn't because when Norman had told him about the plants in Florida, he'd believed him.

Norman blabbed on. "And they went to the kitchen one night on their skateboards, and Stanley opened the refrigerator door to get orange juice, and Fluffy accidentally escaped out of the house and almost got chewed up by the trash truck." He paused to take a breath.

"Wait a minute!" said Dr. Sparks. "In the entire history of the science of botany, there has never been a plant that ate socks—or did any of those other things. If it had happened, somebody would have mentioned it!"

"But you said," Michael pointed out, "that new kinds of plants are discovered all the time, especially in rain forests."

Sarah added, "And some plants do eat things."

"Just insects," said Dr. Sparks, "not articles of clothing!"

Michael said, "Ours don't go for bug meat, just socks and orange juice. They must be vegetarians."

Dr. Sparks asked Mom, "Did all this really happen?"

"Yes, and it hasn't been easy putting up with it," answered Mom.

"All right," said Dr. Sparks. "Start at the beginning, and don't leave anything out."

The boys and Mom told the whole story of the two weird plants. By the time they finished, the logs had burned down to a few glowing embers and a lot of ashes. Norman and Max had fallen asleep on the floor.

* * *

61

Late that night, in the Sparkses' greenhouse, One, Two, Three, Four, Five, and Baby Fluffy grew two inches.

At the agricultural center, the twenty-six newly arrived little plants were waving tiny vines. Some were playfully tussling with each other, but none got pulled out of a pot.

At the motel where they had spent the night before, the twenty-seventh plant had been found behind a chair by the maid who cleaned the room. It was now sitting alone, with no other plants to tussle with, in the lost-and-found box behind the counter in the motel office.

Back home Dad had rolled Stanley and Fluffy into his and Mom's room so he could sleep comfortably in his own bed. He had lugged the TV in from the living room so he could watch in bed and had fallen asleep with it on. In the darkened bedroom, the glow of light from the screen kept flashing different colors as Stanley, who had found the remote control on the bed, kept changing channels.

Chapter 10

After breakfast the next morning Dr. Sparks took them back to the greenhouse complex to check on the new plants.

"I don't see any problems here," she said. "They're all still in their pots. I'll try to arrange for someone to watch them one night this week to see if anything's going on."

Dr. Sparks had some more questions to ask about Fluffy and Stanley. Back at the house they sat around and talked for a long time. They were interrupted by a ding-ding-ding from the direction of the kitchen. Sarah got up. "My stuff in the oven is done," she said. Norman followed her to the kitchen because he wanted a drink of water.

"What are you cooking?" he asked.

"I'll give you a hint. It's brown."

"Brownies?" he guessed.

"No. Guess again."

"Chocolate cake."

"No."

"I give up," said Norman. She turned off the dinging timer, opened the oven, and took out a large flat cake pan full of crumbled brown stuff.

"What is it? Some kind of funny dessert?" asked Norman.

Putting the pan on top of the stove to cool, Sarah replied, "It's dirt."

"Oh, yuck," said Norman. "You cook dirt?"

"For my houseplants," explained Sarah. "Actually it's compost. I bake it at two hundred degrees for thirty minutes. That kills any insects or plant diseases that might be in it. So it's very clean dirt."

Norman was astounded. All he could think of to say was "Oh, yuck," again.

Sarah was enjoying grossing him out. She said, "Of course, if there are any worms in it, I take those out before I put it in the oven. I wouldn't want to bake worms. They're very important to the environment. You know they eat compost and other icky stuff and digest it into excellent soil."

Norman scrunched up his mouth as if he had bitten into a slice of lemon.

Sarah continued, "I know lots of recipes for dirt—what to mix for the best potting soils for different kinds of plants. Compost, peat moss, sand, dried cow manure. I could write down some good dirt recipes for you to take home."

"I don't cook much," he said. "I don't need recipes."

"If you change your mind," said Sarah, grinning, "let me know."

He scooted back to the group in the living room.

When they arrived home late Sunday afternoon, the boys were bubbling over, telling Dad about all the interesting things they had seen and done.

After a while, he asked, "Don't you want to know

64

how your plants got along without you this weekend?"
He told them how Fluffy had followed him across the
hall.

"Did Fluffy miss me?" asked Norman.

"I don't think so," said Dad. "We got along really
well together."

"What about Stanley?" asked Michael.

"He was fine," said Dad, "although I thought he
looked a little tired and droopy this morning. Maybe he
doesn't like TV. I fell asleep and left it on all night."

Mom stood in the dining room door and remarked,
"It's great to be able to use the dining room again
without tripping over a bunch of plants."

"But we hardly ever use it," said Dad, "except to
stack stuff all over the table."

She ignored that. "We'll eat breakfast in here in the
morning," she announced.

Michael had two extra pairs of dirty socks from the
last two days, so after he put out Stanley's regular por-
tion that night, he sealed up the extras in a plastic bag.
That way they would not lose their delicate smell and
he would be prepared in case he ever had to go away
suddenly again.

Because it had been a long day and tomorrow was
Monday, they all went to bed early.

So an hour later, they did not hear a car pull into
their drive. They did not see Jason and his mother get
out and come to the front door. Since the house was
completely dark, the visitors did not ring the bell. They
just put down in front of the door what they were carrying—five more little plants.

Early the next morning Norman was putting cereal
bowls on the dining room table. "It's a relief," said

Mom, "to have all those pesky plants two hundred and fifty miles from here." Then she went to bring in the newspaper and opened the front door. "Oh, no!" she exclaimed.

Norman came running.

Mom said, "What are these doing here?"

Norman suggested helpfully, "Maybe they followed us home."

Mom slammed the door as if to show the plants that she was not going to invite them in.

He continued, "I read this book once where a dog walked for hundreds and hundreds and hundreds of miles to go back home after it got stolen. Its paws got really tired. And it didn't even have a map or know how to read road signs."

Mom said, "Plants can't do that."

"I bet Fluffy could," said Norman, "to get back to me."

She said, "I know they didn't stow away in the car trunk. So the logical explanation is that somebody brought them here last night." She yelled, "Michael! Come here and do something about this."

Michael ambled down the hall, pulling on his T-shirt. Mom opened the door to reveal the new arrivals.

"Oh, no," he said, "Jason must have got back some more that he forgot about." Mom slammed the door again.

Norman told her, "If you keep closing the door on them, they're going to think you don't like them."

"I don't," said Mom.

Michael went out and put them in the garage.

At school Jason came running up to Michael. "Did you find the plants I left last night? My mom said we shouldn't ring the bell because there weren't any lights on."

Michael asked, "Where did they come from? I thought we got them all back."

"They're some I sort of forgot about," explained Jason. "I sold them to some kids when I was visiting my aunt in Elmville. Sunday we went back to my aunt's again, so I talked them into selling them back for only a dollar apiece."

Michael asked, "Did you sell any more that I don't know about?"

"I guess not," he answered.

"You have to be sure," insisted Michael. "Think. Did you sell any more seeds to anybody else?"

"No," said Jason. "That's all I sold."

"You're sure?"

"Yes. What are you going to do with so many little plants anyway? You're going to go broke buying socks when they get bigger!"

"No, we took them over the weekend to that botanist we met in Florida."

"Then the botanist will go broke," said Jason. "By the way," he asked, "how exactly do Stanley and Fluffy eat orange juice?" Michael explained that to him.

When Michael got home from school, the five plants were gone from the garage. He hoped Mom had not started a compost pile. But she told him that she had packed them up in a large box, taken them to a next-day package delivery service, and sent them to Dr. Sparks.

"She'll get them tomorrow," Mom said.

Michael asked, "What did she say? Was she glad to be getting some more?"

"I didn't call her," replied Mom. "I didn't want to give her a chance to say no."

Life got back to normal, or as normal as it could be with Stanley and Fluffy in the family. With enough socks and orange juice keeping them happy, the plants were not causing any trouble.

Michael decided to try to switch the light cycle for Stanley and Fluffy. "That way," he told Norman, "we can see what they're doing in the daytime like Dr. Sparks. We've hardly ever seen them eat socks because they do it while we're asleep. Who knows what else they might be doing?"

Norman agreed to go along, but the plan lasted only one night because Mom looked in to check on them and found them asleep with the lights on. She turned them out. The next morning she asked how they had managed to fall asleep with lights on.

"I had to put a blanket over my head," said Norman.

She pried the plan out of them. Then she said, "Absolutely not! We're not running up the electric bill so you can play with your plants in the daytime. And you wouldn't sleep well with the lights on all night anyway."

"We could put the plants in a different room," said Michael.

Mom replied, "We don't have a room to spare. We're using them all."

"We hardly ever use the dining room," he said. "We could leave those lights on all night. Then in the daytime we could close the drapes and the doors, so it'd be dark in there."

Mom said, "So if we had company over for Sunday dinner, everyone would have to eat with a fork in one hand and a flashlight in the other. That would be a Sunday dinner no one would ever forget.''

Norman offered helpfully, ''I could teach Fluffy to pass the ketchup and mustard.''

''No,'' said Mom. ''How did I get involved in this crazy discussion?''

She noticed that Norman looked really disappointed.

''Besides,'' she said, ''you couldn't have them be active during the day because when you take them to Pet Plant Day in the fall, they'd be acting up all day at school. That would really be a disaster.''

''But we could switch them back to nights in time for that,'' said Michael.

''Then they'd be totally confused,'' Mom pointed out. ''Like people getting jet lag when they fly to far-off time zones. They feel completely out of whack. You don't want to do that to Fluffy and Stanley. They'd be nervous wrecks.''

So the light cycle plan was out. Michael decided instead to teach Stanley something new. He wrapped a couple of vines around his waist and practiced towing his plant up and down the hall and around the house. After many tries, when Michael commanded, ''Hang on,'' Stanley held on firmly even though it wasn't late at night. This turned out to be easier than pushing the plant, so Michael started to haul Stanley around this way often.

They received a thank-you note from Dr. Sparks for the extra plants, along with a check from the research center for all the seeds and plants. They were growing well, she reported, and an overnight watch had revealed some activity. She planned to videotape this and would send them a copy.

Dad said, "I've been wanting to get us a VCR anyway. Now we have a good excuse to buy one."

"I don't think we can afford one right now," said Mom.

"Let's charge it," said Dad, "and pay it off in installments."

Since Dad was in a buying mood, Michael decided to try for a new bike. He had outgrown his old one, and hadn't used it for a long time. Norman had started using it, because he had outgrown his little one.

"I really need a new bike," said Michael. "We could charge it and pay it off in installments."

Dad did not look very interested in this. All he said was "Hmmmm." Michael had a good idea. "We could sell Norman's old bike, and use that money. Then I could earn some more money to help pay the extra cost."

Now Dad looked interested. "You want a new bike that much?" Michael nodded and waited for an answer.

"Okay," said Dad. "First the VCR, then the bike."

Chapter 11

They were ready with a VCR hooked up to the TV when the tape arrived. They all sat down to watch.

The tape began with a picture of a bunch of the little plants, which had grown so much that they could no longer be called little. The lighting was very dim, so it was hard to make out details. Several minutes went by. Nothing happened.

Dad said, "This is about as interesting as watching wallpaper."

Mom said, "Be patient. I'm sure Susan wouldn't have sent this tape if something doesn't happen on it."

Norman said excitedly, "There! I think one moved!"

"Where?" asked Michael.

"Well, I thought I saw it move. Wait! Right there! See that?" A vine twitched. Then it slowly lifted, reached over, and yanked on the plant beside it. That one raised a vine to grab back, and they began tussling.

"See?" said Norman. "I told you they could arm wrestle!"

"This is amazing," said Dad. Soon the other plants began playfully tussling or just waving and stretching their vines. This went on and on and on.

"How long is this tape?" asked Mom.

Dad looked at the box. "Six hours," he replied.

"Hit the fast forward," said Mom.

On the VCR remote control, Michael hit the slow motion button by mistake.

"Great," said Dad. "On slo mo this tape will take twelve hours."

Michael found fast forward. The plants' movement sped up. They were waving around with great energy, like an aerobic exercise class.

This also went on and on and on. Finally something different happened, and Michael slowed the picture down to regular speed. Hands came into the picture, placing white things about the size of Ping-Pong balls around the plants' pots.

"What are those?" asked Mom. "They look like wadded-up balls of paper."

"I think that's what they are," said Michael. "Remember Dr. Sparks's idea about training plants to pick up litter?"

The vines just poked around among the scrunched-up paper balls as if they were trying to figure out what those things were. This went on and on and on. Michael hit fast forward again.

"Aren't they going to do anything else?" asked Norman.

"Call me if anything happens," said Dad. "I'll be in the garage doing stuff I've been putting off doing."

"I didn't know research could be so boring," said Michael, picking up a book.

"It takes a long time," said Mom. "I think you have to have a lot of patience to do research. Does anybody besides me want popcorn?" She headed for the kitchen.

Norman was tired of sitting and went outside to run around to stretch his legs, leaving Michael to keep watch on the tape.

Michael kept glancing up from his book to check if anything new was happening on the screen. Nothing was. Pretty soon he got so interested in his book that he did not glance up very often.

So none of them saw one plant finally manage to pick up a wadded paper and toss it at a nearby plant, which swatted it back. The paper fell down, and the plants all went on waving and poking around at the paper.

After a while Mom came back with a bowl of popcorn. "Anything happen?" she asked.

"Nope," replied Michael. Mom sat staring at the screen until she ran out of popcorn.

"You're right," she said. "This is really boring." She went off to do something else.

Later Dad came back and plopped down on the couch. "I got the garage cleaned up," he announced. "It's a boring job, but not as boring as this tape. Let me know if anything happens. I'll be in the shower."

Michael was tired of being the only one stuck with watching. "Where's Norman?" he asked Dad.

"He went over to Bob's."

Michael called him at Bob's and told him it was his turn to watch the rest of the tape. When Norman got home, Michael handed him the remote control and took off.

After fifteen minutes of more plant waving, Norman fell asleep on the couch. Michael, coming back through the living room, took the remote from his limp little hand and pressed stop. They would have to finish watching it later.

*   *   *

In the next few days Michael tried to think of what he could do to earn money. He knew how to mow a lawn, but Mrs. Smith's son Shawn already had a good summer business doing all the yards in the neighborhood that people wanted help with. Shawn would probably be home from college soon.

Michael decided to tell the neighbors that he was available to do jobs if they needed help, although he wasn't sure what kind of jobs those might be.

He didn't want to ring doorbells and talk to everybody, so he kept thinking he would start doing it the next day. Then he didn't get around to starting.

Dad suggested that he put his message and phone number on paper. So he wrote it out and the next time they went to the library he used the copy machine to make twenty copies. One afternoon after school he took the copies around and left them without ringing doorbells.

Then he waited for phone calls, but nobody called.

He mentioned to Jason that he was planning to get a new bike.

Jason said, "You can get good deals on bikes at garage sales. And read the classified ads in the newspaper. People who want to sell things put ads in there. I got my bike for a really good price from a want ad. New ones at stores cost a lot more." Michael started reading the ads.

Then he got his first phone call for a job. Mrs. DiSanto down the street wanted him to help with her son Ricky's birthday party. He thought a party would be fun, until he got there. First he blew up many, many balloons. Then he spent the next hour running around after ten shrieking, squealing little kids. When cake and ice cream were served, they were more interested in playing with it with their fingers than in eating it. Michael came home exhausted, with tiny chocolate and vanilla fingerprints all over him.

His next job came from Mrs. Smith. She and some other people were making plans for a neighborhood Fourth of July block party with a cookout, games, and a parade. Mrs. Smith hired Michael to deliver flyers to every house in a four-block area. Everyone was being asked to chip in for food and to volunteer for various tasks to make the day fun for everyone.

Mrs. Smith asked Mom to be in charge of getting the permit from the police department to close off four blocks from traffic for the day. "I thought you would be just the person to handle that," said Mrs. Smith, "since you already know the police."

"Now about the parade," she told the boys, "You have to bring your plants. The few times they've been out, not everyone had a chance to see them. It'll be a real treat. They're so spectacular."

Norman said, "Fluffy would love to be in a parade."

Mom said, "Wait a minute."

But Michael said, "It's in the daytime, right?"

"Right," said Mrs. Smith.

"So there won't be any problems with having the plants be in it," he told Mom.

"Problems?" asked Mrs. Smith.

Mom said, "I guess it would be all right. As long as you get them back in the house by nightfall."

"My goodness," remarked Mrs. Smith, laughing. "They don't turn into vampires at sunset, do they?"

"Definitely not vampires," said Michael.

Norman asked, "Are we going to have a band in the parade?"

"No," replied Mrs. Smith. "The only band in this

neighborhood is that bunch who makes such a racket practicing in the Donovans' garage. But they can't play unless their instruments and microphones are plugged in. Fortunately, I don't think they have extension cords long enough to be in a parade!'' She chuckled.

"Can we wear costumes?" asked Norman.

"Yes, costumes help make a parade more festive." Norman's eyes lit up.

"Do you have to wear a costume?" asked Michael, who did not want to.

"No, wear whatever you want," said Mrs. Smith.

At school everybody was getting antsy because school would soon be over for the summer. The principal, Mr. Leedy, gave out a reminder note to take home about Pet Plant Day in the fall.

Michael was looking forward to summer—sleeping a little later in the morning, having fun with his friends, not having to do homework, getting his new bike. After school was out, he would have time to check out garage sales.

He still had no idea how much the kind of bike he wanted would cost.

As soon as Norman found out about selling his too-small little bike and using the money to partly pay for another one for his brother, he was furious. He insisted the money from selling his should go to another bike for himself. He even copied Michael by offering to earn money.

"How?" asked Dad.

"I can put on a show," said Norman, "and sell tickets. Bob can be in it, too. I'll use my gorilla head and sing some songs."

Michael muttered, "If you sing, everybody will ask

for their ticket money back.'' Then he decided not to say any more about it. Opposing Norman's idea would only make him more determined to do it.

Mrs. Smith called Michael to say that she had another job for him. ''I'm going to visit my brother and his family,'' she explained, ''and then I'm going on to Shawn's college graduation. So I'll be gone about two weeks, and he'll come home with me to stay until he finds a job.''

Michael thought she was going to ask him to dogsit Margo, but no. ''You're so good with plants,'' she said, ''that I'm sure you're just the person to plantsit. I'll bring my African violets over to your house Saturday morning.''

Chapter 12

Another progress report arrived from Dr. Sparks. The seeds grown in the dark in daytime and lighted at night had developed the rolled-up, ice-cream-cone-shaped leaves needed to suck up socks.

She had divided them into ten groups of four and was starting them on very small socks. She had organized a team of babies, supplying their parents with tiny socks for the little ones to wear for a day and save for weekly pickup so there would be enough dirty socks for the research.

Some plants were receiving tiny clean socks. A couple had developed a taste for wadded-up papers, but they looked sickly and were not growing as well as the others.

Dr. Sparks said that during the times when the plants usually ate, nearly everyone in the research center came to watch. So they had moved the plants to an observation room with a wall-sized window into the next room. This allowed a crowd to see without disturbing the plants. Some scientists timed their lunch breaks to watch. So on one side of the glass they were stuffing their faces with sandwiches and salads, while on the other side the plants were stuffing their leaves with socks.

An assistant had wired up a sound system to record the schlurps and burps and put a speaker in the observation room so the watchers could listen. It was only a one-way sound system, so the plants were not startled by the occasional burps of lunching botanists.

Dr. Sparks said she was sending an audiotape of the noises. She enclosed a note from Sarah. She and her brother had taken naps and gone to bed early one night, setting alarm clocks. Then they got up and watched while their plants ate socks. This was thrilling, she said. One, Two, Three, Four, and Five were growing big on socks. Baby Fluffy was even bigger, too big to be called Baby any more, so Max had renamed it Norman. Sarah said she wasn't sure why Max's plant had grown larger than the others. The only thing he was doing differently was singing to it.

Norman said, "I wonder what song."

The audiotape came in the mail the next day. After a minute of listening to this forty-plant weird noise orchestra, the whole family was laughing like crazy.

It was a symphony of schlurps. Since so many plants were making these noises, one would start and another would chime in, almost as if they were trying to sing in harmony. The last part of the tape turned into a burp concert. Michael laughed so hard for so long that his sides ached.

He wanted to let some some of his friends listen to the tape. He thought there would be no problem if he didn't tell them who was making the noises, but Mom said no.

So Michael just daydreamed about organizing the plants into a band called the Schlurpburps, getting a recording contract, and making a zillion dollars from tapes and CDs.

On Saturday morning, Mrs. Smith called to ask Michael to come over to help her carry the African violets. As he went out, Mom said, "I cleared a little space for them on the dining room table."

Mrs. Smith opened her door and handed him a cardboard box with four plants in it. She picked up another box and walked along with him. After they unloaded them, Michael shoved the boxes under the table.

"No, bring those along," said Mrs. Smith. "We need them to carry the rest."

"How many are there?" he asked.

"Forty-two," she replied.

"Why do you have so many?"

"I guess I just got carried away. Somebody gave me a couple. Then I bought some different varieties, and started some more from leaf cuttings. Then I joined an African violet club and won some ribbons at their annual show. Things sort of took off from there."

After four more trips, Mrs. Smith's plants covered the dining room table and part of the floor. The big and small frilly blossoms were purple, pink, red, and white.

"Be sure not to use cold water," she said. "That chills them and makes white spots if it gets on the leaves."

"Okay," said Michael.

"Run a lot of water ahead of time and let it sit until it's room temperature."

"Okay."

"Don't water until the soil feels dry. Stick your finger in each one, like this."

"Okay." Michael thought this was turning out to be awfully complicated.

"And then water slowly into the plant tray under the pots, so it soaks up from the bottom. Watering too much can make them rot, but I don't think you could do that much damage in only two weeks."

"Okay."

"Of course, not watering enough will make them wilt. So be sure to keep checking them. They'll all be getting dry at different times."

Michael spent the next two weeks sticking his fingers into the dirt around the forty-two plants, trying to decide when they were dry enough to need water, and worrying that he might wreck them with too much water or not enough.

So he was glad to see Mrs. Smith, Margo, and Shawn getting out of Shawn's old car in their driveway. He walked over to say hi and ask if he could bring the plants over right away. Margo was so excited to be home that she nearly knocked Michael over.

"Margo, sit!" commanded Mrs. Smith. Margo sat. Michael wished he could do that to Norman to make him stop doing irritating things. Thinking about it made him smile.

"Shawn will help you bring the violets," said Mrs. Smith.

As they walked to Michael's house, Shawn said, "My mom told me about your weird plants. I'd like to see them."

Michael showed him Stanley and Fluffy. "Amazing," said Shawn. "I've never seen anything like these."

Norman bounded in. "This one's mine," he said proudly and started talking a mile a minute.

Michael did not like Norman horning in. As they started out of the room, he turned and said, "Norman."

"What?"

"Sit!"

Of course, it didn't work. Norman tagged along, talking to Shawn and hogging the attention. He insisted on helping to carry the plants to the Smiths'. When they returned for the last load, he lost interest and stayed home.

Michael helped Shawn unload all the stuff from his car. From the luggage rack on top, Shawn lifted down a bicycle.

"This is a great bike," said Michael with admiration.

"I'm going to sell it after I get a new one soon," said Shawn. "You interested?"

"Yes!" said Michael.

"Take it for a ride," offered Shawn. "See how you like it." Michael hopped on and pedaled away. The bike was deluxe, even better than what he had hoped to buy. When he returned, Shawn was still unloading because the back seat had been packed to the window tops.

Michael asked, "How much do you want for this?"

"I haven't figured that out yet. I'll have to let you know."

The first day after school was out, Michael slept late, hung out with Chad, and watched Shawn mow a lawn down the street.

The next day Mom said, "Okay, enough goofing off. You have to plan some constructive things to do." So he signed up for a pool pass, soccer lessons, and the summer reading program at the library, which was offering pizza coupons for every twenty books read.

Mom put him and Norman to work doing house chores and pulling weeds in the backyard to clear space for growing parsley, peppers, tomatoes, and lettuce.

All this still left Michael time to enjoy dawdling over breakfast, climbing a low tree in the backyard, and just sitting there thinking, watching birds, and listening to the leaves rustle. He hung out with Chad a lot, and once in a while Jason came over to see Stanley and Fluffy. Sometimes the family ate dinner in the backyard. The long summer days seemed to fly by.

Mom talked to her mother every week as usual, but nothing was happening with grandma's plant. She left a sock out, now and then, but it was always still there in the morning.

Then one morning during breakfast the phone rang, and Norman answered it. "It's Grandma," he announced. "She says last night her plant squeezed toothpaste all over itself and the bathroom sink!"

Mom got on the phone. When she hung up, Dad asked, "Is she upset enough to give up the plant?"

"She's not upset," replied Mom. "She's delighted. She can hardly wait to see what it's going to do next."

A couple of times when Shawn had to go out of town for job interviews, he asked Michael to take care of some of his yard work customers who couldn't wait until he got back. Michael was glad to earn the extra money. Then Shawn told him he had ordered his new bike and it would be delivered at the beginning of July. So Michael could buy his old one then. They agreed on the price.

Everyone in the neighborhood was starting to get organized for the Fourth of July block party. Norman kept going over to Bob's and wouldn't tell Michael what he was up to.

Shawn stopped by one afternoon to ask Michael if he would like to take over some of his customers. "I got the job in computer software sales that I wanted," he explained, "and I'm moving to Elmville. My yard work is practically a full-time summer job, so I got another guy who's in college to take it over, but I thought you might like to take over a few. You interested?"

Michael jumped at the chance. Shawn took him around to four homes in the neighborhood, talked to the owners about Michael taking his place, and walked him around the yards to show him what needed to be done. He was all set to start after the Fourth of July.

As time went on, they began receiving amazing progress reports from Grandma about her plant. On various mornings she awoke to find that it had pumped hand lotion all over the floor, plucked all the tissues from a box and flung them in every direction, and unrolled all the toilet paper.

Michael deduced that it must be looking for something to eat and didn't like the taste of hand lotion, tissues, or toilet paper. So he told her on the phone, "I think it needs socks."

"I tried socks a few times and nothing happened."

"Hmmm," said Michael. "What color were they?"

"Navy blue," replied Grandma.

"That must be the problem," he said. "Try pink. And do you have any white ones with brown stripes?"

"I could buy some."

Michael said, "Make sure they're really dirty. Like, wear the same ones for two or three days."

84

Grandma called back in three days to tell him his advice had worked.

After she started providing dirty socks in the most delicious colors, her plant settled down and stopped making messes. But after she went away on a trip for four days, she returned to find it had dragged itself into the shower, trying to water itself. Its vines were wrapped around the faucets, but hadn't been able to turn them on.

A week later, it learned to flush the toilet, apparently just for fun. It was doing it so often that Grandma decided to move the plant into her bedroom to keep her water bill from skyrocketing.

There it behaved itself, satisfied with socks. Grandma told Mom, "I've had enough interesting things happen. I guess I won't buy that skateboard after all."

Chapter 13

On the morning of the Fourth of July, Michael took Stanley into the kitchen and washed his leaves. Then he oiled the skateboard wheels to make the plant easier to push in the parade.

Norman poked his head in and said in a bossy tone, "Don't forget the parade meeting in Mrs. Smith's yard!"

Michael did not respond. He hated it when Norman tried to tell him what to do.

Norman yelled, "Hurry up! It's right now!"

Michael said casually, "I'll be there in a little while."

"Now!" nagged Norman. "It's starting now!"

Michael sighed. Now he would have to wait even longer before he went over there, just to show Norman.

The front door banged.

Michael watched the clock for five really boring minutes. Then he set out for Mrs. Smith's. On the way he met Shawn, who was carrying a cardboard box that looked heavy.

"I'm leaving early this afternoon," Shawn explained. He added with a grin, "But not until after the food."

"You won't be able to get your car out then," Michael said. "The picnic's going to be all over the street."

"I already parked way down the street early this morning," said Shawn, "past the barriers where they blocked it off. But I didn't get up early enough to pack the car, so I have to lug all my stuff down there."

"I can help," said Michael.

"Thanks," said Shawn. "Hey, I'm not going to load my new bike until the last. Would you like to ride it in the parade?"

"That would be great!" replied Michael. "I can help you after the parade."

"After the food," said Shawn, laughing.

In Mrs. Smith's backyard, Michael found her explaining to a crowd what order everyone was going to march in. She had a big chart propped up with a list on it.

Michael saw that he and Stanley were supposed to march right after the antique car. But he couldn't do that and ride Shawn's magnificent bike in the parade's bike unit—not unless he walked with Stanley first and then ran back to get in with the bikes. Then he got a better idea.

He was staring at the list when he realized that on the schedule right between the parade and the picnic was an unexpected event to take place at his family's garage—a show by Norman and Bob.

Flags hung outside houses all along the street. The parade formed around a corner so no part could be seen before it rounded the corner and turned on the four-block marching route.

Leading off were three teenage girls carrying big

flags. They were followed by a boy pulling a wagon with a boom box in it that was blasting toe-tapping marching music.

Then came the two youngest Kramer girls, Mary and Ashley, who had been taking twirling lessons. Their sequined outfits sparkled in the sun. They pointed their batons left and then right, up and then down. The tassels on their boots flopped about smartly with every step. Once in a while they would stop to twirl their batons. They only dropped them a few times.

Then came all the neighborhood babies and toddlers being pushed in strollers, pulled in wagons, or carried by proud parents. One baby was wearing a red, white, and blue diaper. Another, with a sun hat and sun glasses, waved his chubby fists in time to the music pouring from another boom box.

A little girl walked by with a round thing on her head with prongs sticking out of it. She was wrapped in a green piece of cloth and holding up a flashlight. "The Statue of Liberty," explained her mother to everyone within earshot. The watchers lining the curbs clapped and cheered for all the marchers.

Following the Statue of Liberty came another amazing sight—Fluffy, pushed by Norman and Bob. Such a large, strange plant would have been a center of attention in any parade, but the boys had gone all out to make an impression. With their blue jeans, Norman was wearing a red T-shirt and Bob a white one. Topping off their outfits were Norman's gorilla head and Bob's Frankenstein head, plus baseball hats with little flags taped on the brims.

Norman had insisted on an outfit for Fluffy, too. They had raided Bob's mother's gift wrapping supplies and tied red, white, and blue bows all over the plant. On the front of Fluffy's pot was propped a tape recorder playing Kermit the Frog singing, "It's Not That Easy Being Green." On the back of the pot was a sign advertising their show.

They got almost as many cheers as the little Statue of Liberty. Norman, a true ham, waved happily to the onlookers with his free hand.

A neighbor standing next to Dad remarked, "I've never seen a plant marching in a parade before."

Dad replied, "It's sort of like an ecology float, but not exactly."

Next appeared many kids riding slowly along on their bicycles, which they had decorated with crepe paper woven through their wheel spokes. Some had streamers trailing from handlebars.

Then came a gleaming red convertible, a classic car, driven by a neighborhood man who owned it. His family sat in the front and back seats and waved. Also in the back seat was their golden retriever, who sat there just like another person.

Now there was a long blank space in the parade. Just when people were starting to wonder if it was over, around the corner came Michael, proudly riding Shawn's magnificent bike and towing Stanley. Some of the plant's vines were wrapped around his waist. The rest were wrapped around the bike frame under the seat.

Michael kept glancing back over his shoulder, just to reassure himself that Stanley was doing okay. The plant looked wonderful. His polished leaves gleamed in the sun and fluttered a little as they sailed slowly along.

As they turned the corner onto the parade route, the watchers began to clap and cheer like crazy. Out of the

89

corner of his left eye, Michael saw Stanley swinging out wide to the left behind the bike—like a water-skier on a towrope.

Michael knew that if he stopped suddenly the plant would keep rolling and maybe slam into the bike or the crowd. So he kept going straight, hoping Stanley would get back in line. The plant did, but then veered way to the right. The crowd went wild at the great stunt they thought Michael was doing on purpose.

Michael calmed down. At least he was sure now that the plant was not going to crash into the crowd. In response to the cheers, he wanted to look like he knew what he was doing, so he let go of one handlebar and waved.

To his astonishment, he felt Stanley's vines let go of his waist. He glanced back, expecting to see the plant running amok. But Stanley, still holding on to the bike frame, was rolling behind him, waving a couple of vines. Was he waving at the crowd? If he was, Michael thought, nobody would realize it because the vines just looked as if they were blowing in the breeze.

They made it to the end of the parade route. Michael was wondering how to stop the bike and Stanley at the same time, when Dad caught up with him and stopped the plant so Michael could stop the bike. Dad walked the bike back to Shawn's house and left Michael to push Stanley home. On the way people kept stopping him to get a closer look at the plant.

Norman came running up. "I need Stanley to be in my show," he said.

"Use Fluffy," replied Michael.

"I need them both," said Norman, "to be a jungle."

Michael continued rolling his plant toward home.

"Who else is in this show?" he asked. "Just you and Bob?"

"And a girl," said Norman.

"Who?"

"I don't know yet. I have to get one."

"How is somebody going to be in a show that starts in a few minutes without practicing?"

"I'll tell her what to do as we go along," said Norman confidently. "I need you to run the garage door opener. Okay?"

"Why not," agreed Michael. Norman dashed off to find a girl.

Chapter 14

A crowd of families gathered in the driveway with their chairs facing the closed garage door. Michael leaned near the door waiting for Norman's signal. Finally he heard from inside, "Okay, raise the curtain."

Michael pressed the opener and walked around to the side of the crowd to watch. The garage door slowly rattled up on its tracks, revealing Fluffy and Stanley in front of the back end of the car. Its back window was covered with taped-together newspaper so no one could see in. Both car doors stood open.

From the left one bounded Norman, wearing his gorilla head and growling loudly. He made grabbing motions at the plants' leaves and pretended to eat some of them. "Yum, yum," he shouted, "These plants really taste good." Then he bounded around back into the other car door.

A moment later he popped out the other side wearing his glasses with the moustache and funny nose from his detective kit, plus his baseball hat and a backpack.

"What a nice day for a walk in the jungle!" he exclaimed. "It seems like nothing ever happens in the jungle when you're a botanist and you're out for a walk minding your own business.''

He turned to Fluffy and threw up his hands. ''What's been eating this plant?'' he cried. ''It looks like a gorilla has been here! I wish they'd eat peanut butter sandwiches like everybody else and leave plants alone!''

Michael watched in amazement. He looked around at the rest of the audience to see how they were taking all this. They looked pretty amazed, too, but they were all smiling.

Norman walked back and forth in front of the plants a few times. Nothing happened. He went around to the left car door and whispered loudly, ''Now!''

Out came little Ashley Kramer. She was struggling with a large towel wrapped around the waist of her spangled twirler outfit like a long skirt. It kept sagging, and she kept tripping on it.

Norman whispered instructions to her.

''Help! Help!'' she said. Michael thought she wanted help with her towel skirt, but she added, ''Frankenstein and King Kong are after me!''

Norman inquired politely, ''What are you doing out here in the jungle?'' He leaned over and whispered to her.

''A what?'' she said. He whispered again.

''I'm a botan-what?'' she asked.

''IST! IST!'' he informed her. ''What a coincidence! So am I.''

From the car lunged Bob wearing his Frankenstein head and walking stiffly with arms outstretched.

Norman whispered to Ashley. ''Oh, no,'' she said. ''Here comes Frankenstein!''

Norman whipped off his nose and glasses. ''This is

93

a job for Sockman!'' he shouted and ran back into the car. Bob chased Ashley back and forth in front of the plants. Once in a while they would stop and stand there, and then start going back and forth again.

"Sockman, hurry up!" said Bob.

Norman emerged again. This time he was wearing a pair of Dad's big knee socks over the legs of his jeans. On his hands he wore another pair of socks. Pinned around his neck were the corners of an extra large red bath towel, which hung down his back and dragged behind him on the garage floor. He was waving his Blaster.

Frankenstein asked, "Who are you?"

"I'm Sockman!" he announced. The audience clapped and cheered. He yelled "To the rescue!" and put the Blaster on the floor so he could get both hands on Frankenstein.

"I don't need weapons," Sockman told the audience. "I'm the forces of good."

He and Frankenstein grabbed each other. They leaned together to the left and then to the right, going "Uh! Uh! Uh!" They did this several times.

Forgetting to whisper, Norman said, "Lie down." Bob let go of him and stretched out on the floor with his arms sticking up in the air.

"Okay, Frankenstein," said Sockman. "Will you be good now?"

"Yes, I'll be good."

"You promise?"

"Yes, yes!"

"Okay, you can get up."

Norman whispered to Ashley. She looked puzzled, but she hitched up her skirt and said, "Thank you, Sockman. You saved me from Frankenstein and King Kong. You're a super market."

94

"You mean super hero," said Sockman, looking irked.

"Okay," said Ashley, smiling happily.

"Wait a minute," said Sockman. He reached into the car and brought out two pairs of socks.

"Put these on your hands," he instructed. They fumbled around trying to do that.

Ashley put one fudge ripple sock on top of the car trunk while she slipped the other one on her arm. Norman was trying to help her, so at first he did not notice Fluffy sneaking out a vine behind them.

But then from the corner of his eye he saw a sock flashing through the air. Norman grabbed, caught the toe of the sock, and yanked. Fluffy yanked back. This all happened so fast that the audience gasped with surprise. Then they laughed and applauded as Sockman and Fluffy kept up the tug-of-war. Small children shrieked with delight.

"How does he do that?" asked one child loudly.

"It's a trick," explained a boy sitting nearby. "There's somebody hiding behind the plant making it do that. Like a puppet."

"But I don't see any hands or strings," said a small girl.

"It has to be a magic trick," said her mother. "Plants can't do things like that by themselves."

Sockman won the tug by unwinding the vine from the sock. He pulled Ashley as far from the plants as possible, and helped her put the rescued sock on her hand.

"I now pronounce you Sockwoman," he said. Turning to Frankenstein, he said, "I now pronounce you Sockenstein."

"Oh, thank you, Sockman," said the monster. "I'll

never bother botanists again. Or plants either. And neither will King Kong.''

Norman stepped in front of them and raised his sock-clad hands. ''When you put your socks on,'' he said, ''you are the forces of good. Not as good as me, but almost.''

Everyone applauded. He leaned over, bowing to the audience. He waved at Michael to bring down the door and kept bobbing up and down. Michael pressed the button. Since he was standing near the back of the crowd, he did not notice that the Blaster, still on the floor, was lying in the way. Norman was so enchanted with the applause that he did not notice either.

The door came down hard on the middle of the Blaster, splattering a mighty blast of mustard right at Norman.

When Michael sent the door back up for their curtain call, Norman was staring down at his feet and legs, which were covered with big yellow splotches. Since he had been leaning way over when the mustard hit, there was some on top of his head. It was starting to dribble down his forehead.

Bob had pulled off his Frankenstein head and was laughing like crazy. Ashley took off her towel skirt and helpfully offered it to Norman. The crowd clapped wildly.

Lots of people came up to tell the actors how much they liked the show. One kid who had been in the front row said, ''The tug-of-war with the plant was good, but the yellow goo at the end was great!''

''How did you do that with the plant?'' someone asked. ''It looked like it was really hanging on to that sock!'' A group was gathered around Norman, looking eager for the answer.

Norman opened his mouth to reply, but no words came out because he didn't know what to say.

Michael spoke up quickly. "Special effects," he said, "amazing special effects. I bet you never saw anything like that before, did you?" The people gathered around agreed that they never had.

Mrs. Smith told Norman, "That was the best show I've ever seen!"

Dad told him he did a wonderful job. Mom said, "I'm so proud of you. Your show was a big hit with everybody." She added, "Don't go in the house until I hose you down."

"I forgot to sing my song," said Norman.

"Don't worry about it," said Dad. "You had a big enough ending."

Mom asked, "What on earth were you doing with mustard in your Water Blaster?"

Norman explained, "Mrs. Smith said I could squirt it on the hamburgers and hot dogs at the food table. She said everybody would think it was cute."

"Are you sure this was her idea?" asked Mom suspiciously.

"Not exactly," said Norman. He added, "I washed the Blaster out real good with hot soapy water before I put the mustard in."

"Well, okay," said Mom. "I'm sure you'll be the talk of the picnic."

As she wiped mustard out of his hair, Norman complained, "I wish the Blaster pointed the other way."

Mom said, "Just be glad you didn't get the audience. You've gotten enough people with that thing already."

"Not too many," he protested. "That TV lady who interviewed us about our plants wasn't my fault. If she hadn't grabbed the front end of my Blaster, she wouldn't have got maple syrup all over her shoes."

Mom added, "And her skirt. Then you got Susan Sparks in Florida with the grape jelly."

"I thought she was attacking my plant, so I was just attacking her back."

Mom said, "It seems only fair that this time you got yourself with some goo." She tickled his ribs and said, "You smell like a hot dog." They both started to giggle.

The whole neighborhood was starting to smell delicious with food grilling outdoors. People were setting up long tables in the street with casseroles, baked beans, fruits, vegetables, and yummy desserts.

Norman changed clothes and ran off with his Blaster to take up his post next to the five gallon jar of ketchup, which had a pump dispenser. He was a such a big hit providing squirts of mustard that he had to refill the Blaster several times. Fortunately his aim was pretty good. He scored bulls-eyes on most of the hamburgers and hot dogs held out to him. Only a few people wound up with mustard on their fingers or shoelaces.

People brought their own chairs out in the street and ate, balancing plates on their laps. Some even brought out high chairs for their babies.

Up the block at the Donovans' the band plugged in, rolled up the garage door, and started blasting away. As people finished eating, many followed the music to dance in the driveway and street.

"May I have this dance?" Dad asked Mom.

"Let's boogie," she replied. They headed up the street to join in.

Michael wandered around. He saw some neighbors

he had never seen before. Those he had not seen for a long time all told him he had grown. It was fun being able to walk around in the street without cars.

He heard Shawn call his name and went over to the Smiths' front yard. "Ready to help load?" asked Shawn.

They made many trips. Shawn was apparently taking everything he owned. After the trunk was filled, they put stuff in the back seat until it was almost full to the roof, covering up the back window. Then they tied a few things to the luggage rack on top of the car.

Shawn attached a new bike rack to the back of the trunk. "That's everything but the bike," he said. They strolled back to his house. "I'm going to miss the old neighborhood," said Shawn. "But I'm really looking forward to my new job and being on my own."

Mary Kramer came up to Michael. "Are you going to take your plant out again today?" she asked.

"Why do you want to know?" asked Michael.

"My grandpa's sick and doesn't get out much. We did our baton act in his room for him, but he had to watch the rest of the parade from his window. He loves plants, and he said he wished he could get a better look at yours because he's never seen anything like it. So I wondered if you were going to take your plant out maybe you could bring it over to his window. I think it would cheer him up."

"Yeah, I could do that," said Michael. The Kramers lived down near where Shawn had parked his car. "I was going that way anyway," he said. He told Shawn, "I'll get my plant and walk back to the car with you."

By the time he rolled Stanley out, Shawn was out front with his bike and his mother. When they all got to the car, Shawn locked the bike on the new rack. Now he was all set to go. His mother hugged him. He shook hands with Michael.

Shawn got into the driver's seat, cranked up his stereo to ear-splitting volume, waved goodbye, rolled up the window, and drove away.

As Michael stood there waving at the back of the car, Stanley rolled past him.

Chapter 15

"Oh, my goodness," exclaimed Mrs. Smith. "Your plant seems to be caught on the bike."

Stanley, whose vines were wrapped around the bike, was happily rolling away into the distance.

"Stop!" Michael yelled to Shawn, who could not hear him and could not see he was being trailed by a plant.

"Let go!" he yelled to Stanley, who had practiced "Hang on!" but not "Let go!"

Michael panicked. His new bike was several houses away in the garage. The street was filled with tables, chairs, and people, so nobody could get a car out fast without moving all those obstacles.

Mrs. Smith said, "I'll try to find your parents and call the police to stop the car."

Michael realized that unless he did something immediately, Stanley was headed for disaster.

Michael yelled to a girl leaning on a bike nearby, "Can I borrow your bike? My plant's getting away!"

She handed it over. He heard Norman shouting behind him, "What happened?" He must have run into Mrs. Smith.

Michael mounted the bike and shouted back at Norman, "Stanley's getting towed out of town by Shawn's car! Get help!" He sped away. Stanley was already out of sight.

Norman ran home and got Michael's old bike out. Bob came running up. "Where are you going?" he asked.

"Stanley's getting dragged away! I have to help my brother go to the rescue! Go find my mom and dad and tell them where we went!"

Bob ran off to hunt for them. Norman decided to leave a note in case Bob couldn't find them. Then he took off after Michael.

While Bob and Mrs. Smith were looking for them on one side of the street, Mom and Dad were strolling home on the other side. As they came up the front walk, Dad said, "What's that by the door? It looks like somebody wrote something there."

Mom wiped a finger at one of the letters, smelled it, and announced, "It's a message in mustard."

The yellow lettering said, "HELP S ESCAPE COME QUICK NO."

"Come quick no?" said Dad. "What does that mean?"

"This is definitely Norman's printing," said Mom, "so 'no' must be short for Norman. He must have been in a big hurry."

"What about help S escape? Who are we supposed to help escape?" wondered Dad.

"The only S I can think of is Stanley. Maybe Stanley escaped like Fluffy did that time. I'll check in the house." She came back out in a flash. "Stanley's gone," she said. "But where?"

102

"Look," said Dad pointing. A line of yellow went across the grass and into the street.

"He made a trail with the Blaster for us to follow," said Mom. But Dad had already figured that out and was getting Michael's new bike out of the garage. "We can't get the car out in the street," he said. "I'll have to go by bike."

Dad, who had not been on a bike in years, wobbled off down the street in not very hot pursuit, dodging tables, chairs, and people.

Mom ran into the garage. The only thing with wheels left in there besides the car and lawn mower was Norman's little outgrown bicycle. She sat down on it. It was much too low for her, but she didn't let that stop her. Off she pedaled, pumping hard with her knees nearly bumping her chin, following the yellow goo trail.

In the meantime, Shawn had noticed that his gas gauge was on empty, so he pulled into the first gas station he saw and turned off the motor at the gas pump. He was very surprised to see Stanley go by. The plant had swung out to the left as the car turned, let go of the bike, and sailed by down the street.

Shawn turned the ignition key to start the car to chase the plant, but it would not start. He leaped out, pumped a dollar's worth of gas so he could get going, ran into the station, found he had left his wallet in the car, went out to get it, ran back in to pay the dollar, and ran back out again.

By now Stanley was nowhere to be seen, but Michael came riding by. When Shawn yelled to get his attention, he swerved into the station lot.

"Where's my plant?" he asked, breathing hard.

"It went that way," replied Shawn, pointing. "What's it doing this far from the neighborhood, and how can it be moving around on its own? I thought you had it with you when I left."

"I did," said Michael. "The vines were wrapped around your bike, so you were towing it. Could you help me search?"

"Sure," said Shawn. "Don't worry. It can't have rolled far without the car pulling it. I'll drive ahead and find it. When you catch up, you can tow it home with the bike if you don't mind because I have to get going. And I have to get more gas."

"Thanks," said Michael. He rode away in the direction Shawn had indicated, straight down the road. Then Shawn passed him with the car and got far ahead.

Soon Michael realized that the car, now off in the distance, had gone much, much farther than Stanley could possibly have rolled. This road did not slant downhill, so the plant should have come to a stop.

Shawn had obviously figured this out, too, because Michael saw the car coming back.

"It can't have gotten this far," Shawn said when he pulled up. "I don't know how, but we must have gone by it and not seen it." They headed back towards the gas station with Shawn scanning the right side of the road and Michael the left. There was no sign of Stanley.

As they neared the station, Michael saw Norman. He was aiming his Blaster down at the sidewalk.

"Where's Dad and Mom?" yelled Michael.

"I couldn't find them," called Norman, "so I came to the rescue myself and left a message for them to come after us!"

Michael got closer and saw that Norman was squeezing a line of mustard onto the sidewalk. Had he gone crazy?

"This is a plant emergency!" shouted Michael, "not a play-with-mustard party!"

Norman explained indignantly, "I'm making an arrow once every block for them to follow us!" He added two little lines to make a V at the end of the big line. "See?"

"Oh," said Michael.

Norman gloated, "Great master plan, isn't it?"

Michael replied, "Not too bad."

Shawn pulled up by the curb and got out. Norman told Michael, "Here's Shawn. But Stanley's not with him."

"I know that!" said Michael. "I found him and his car at a gas station, but Stanley let go and rolled past him before I got there. Now we can't find Stanley even though he can't have rolled far. This road isn't downhill," he added so Norman would understand why this was not like their last runaway plant episode.

A police car that had been cruising by suddenly pulled up behind Shawn's car. The officer got out and said, "Shawn Smith?"

"Yes," said Shawn, puzzled about why the man would know his name.

"Your mother called," said the officer, "and asked us to stop you because you left for another city with a large valuable plant she said doesn't belong to you."

Shawn said, "I don't think you got that exactly right."

"Where is it?" asked the officer.

"We're looking for it," replied Shawn. "It got loose and got lost."

"Oh, really?" said the officer.

Michael said, "That's right. It's my plant. It got its vines stuck on the bike on the rack on Shawn's car. He didn't mean to take it. He didn't even know it was there."

"The plant is on rollers," explained Shawn. "So when its vines came loose from my car, it rolled away while I was out of gas. That's why I couldn't go after it right away. Then Michael caught up with me, and we both started searching."

Michael stepped forward. "I want to file a missing plant report," he said, "so the police can be on the lookout for it."

"Yes, please," said Norman, who considered himself an expert because he had watched plenty of police shows on TV. "We need an all points bulletin, and maybe a search party, and if that doesn't work, the FBI."

The officer grinned. "We don't do missing plants," he said, "unless they've been stolen. And the Fourth of July is one of our busiest days of the year. So if you don't find it today," he told Michael, "have your parents come down to headquarters tomorrow and file a lost property report. Then if anybody finds it and calls in, we can let you know."

"And you," he told Shawn, "call your mother." He drove away.

Shawn said, "The nearest phone must be at the gas station. Maybe you guys better call your mother, too."

But that wasn't necessary because as they reached the station, along came Dad, now wobbling less, followed by Mom, pumping like crazy on the little bike.

When Norman shouted to them, they stopped pedaling and coasted into the gas station.

"That was brilliant of you to leave a trail," Mom told Norman, "also a gooey mess, but brilliant." Norman beamed with pride.

The boys explained the situation. Dad decided they should fan out on foot along the road to see if they could find anyone who had seen the plant because it had to be nearby. Maybe someone had found it and taken it home. The attendant let them leave the car and bikes at the station.

Mom remarked to Dad, "On the way home, we're swapping bikes."

"No," said Dad, "we're calling a cab."

Chapter 16

They decided that Michael would go with Dad, Norman would go with Mom, Shawn would go on his own, and they would meet back at the station in half an hour.

Ordinarily Michael would have felt like a fool ringing doorbells and asking strangers if they had seen a large plant on rollers. But he was so worried about Stanley that he didn't care. Besides, Dad was doing most of the asking.

There was no answer at several houses because people were away for the holiday. At one they heard voices coming from the backyard and found a picnic going on. But no one they talked to had seen the plant.

After about twenty minutes, they started trudging back toward the station. Seeing Michael's downcast expression, Dad said, "Don't get discouraged yet. Maybe Shawn, or your mother and Norman found him."

But then they saw Mom and Norman in the distance. There was no plant with them. When they all reached the station, Shawn had not yet returned.

"Any luck?" asked the attendant.

They all said no.

"Maybe the other guy is finding the plant right

108

now," said the attendant helpfully. "Don't give up hope. Hey," he said, pointing, "here he comes!"

Shawn was alone, but he was running and waving. "I found somebody who saw it," he called.

"Who? Where?" they all asked.

"At the second house I went to, a woman told me she looked out her window and saw this big plant standing in the road and a girl standing next to it, looking at it. She assumed the plant belonged to the girl. Later, when she looked out again, they were both gone."

"Does she know who this girl is and where we can find her?" asked Dad.

"No, she never saw her before, but I got a description. About ten or eleven, red hair, blue T-shirt, jeans, and red-white-and-blue streamers on her handlebars.

"She had a bike?" asked Michael, getting a sinking feeling.

"Yeah," said Shawn, "pointed that way so she must have been heading in that direction."

Michael said, "She must have towed him away."

Shawn looked puzzled. "Why does this plant keep getting tangled up with bicycles? It's not safe around one!"

Dad said, "At least we know which way to go to search now."

Shawn said, "I already went to every house for three blocks that way on both sides. Nobody else saw them. And she could have turned left or right off that street at any block."

"They could be anywhere by now," said Mom. "Let's call the police."

"We already tried the police," said Michael. "They said come to the station tomorrow if we don't find Stanley by then."

"Norman told me," said Mom. "But they probably didn't take you seriously because you asked for an APB and a search party."

Norman reminded her, "And the FBI."

Michael protested, "I didn't say those dumb things, he did."

Dad said, "Let's go to the police station now. If we discuss it with them sensibly, I think we'll get better results than just calling up. When they see us, they'll take us seriously."

"How are we going to get there?" asked Norman. They all turned toward Shawn.

"But my car's stuffed full with all my stuff," he said. "There's only enough room in it for me."

"We'll help you unload," said Mom. "And this nice man will take care of your things until you get back." The attendant agreed.

Dad offered to pay for filling up Shawn's gas tank.

At the police station, the group marched up to the officer at the desk. Dad announced, "We have a problem."

"Yes?" said the officer. She looked down at Norman, who was holding his Blaster. It was leaking a little mustard.

"What's he doing with that thing?" she asked. "Is that yellow paint?"

"Don't worry," said Mom, "it's only mustard. For hot dogs. At an unusually big picnic. I'll wipe it up." She started rummaging in her pockets for some tissues.

"The reason I asked," said the officer, "is that we've had a couple of odd calls about gooey yellow arrows painted on sidewalks." She laughed. "I thought maybe you'd captured the phantom arrow graffiti artist."

"No," said Dad firmly. "We need your help to find a red-haired girl on a bicycle last seen with a tall plant on a skateboard about an hour ago on Reynolds Road."

"Is this a member of your family?" asked the officer.

"The plant, not the girl," said Dad. He described them both and explained that the plant had been accidentally towed away and that the girl who found it might have taken it home.

The officer replied, "Then maybe her family called in to report your plant was found. Let me check." She went back to talk to the people answering phones and came back with a couple of papers. "The only odd things we've had reported found in the last hour were those painted yellow arrows. But speaking of plants, here's a report from a man who called in and said his daughter was chased by a giant plant." She shook her head. "We get a lot of weird calls."

Michael said, "Was she riding a bike at the time?"

"As a matter of fact, she was," replied the officer. "It says here that the faster she rode, the faster the plant chased her. It stayed right behind her for several blocks."

"Is it at her house now?" asked Michael.

"No, this says she finally escaped from it. In this job I thought I'd heard everything, but this is a first."

"Could we have their phone number and address?" asked Mom.

"We'd like to check it out," said Dad. "Maybe it's our plant and she's slightly mistaken about the being chased part."

A man came over from the telephone area. "Are you the same family that had a runaway plant two or three months ago?" he inquired.

"Er, yes," said Dad.

111

"Everybody in the department heard about that one," said the man, "and about how you had to walk it home in your pajamas." He smiled. "So your plant got away again?"

"No," said Norman indignantly. "That was my plant. This lost one is my brother's."

"You have two of those big ones?"

Dad nodded. "Can we have that address and phone number?" he asked. "If we can find out where the girl got away from the plant, maybe that's where it is."

The officer wrote down the information for him. "Give us a call if you find it," she said. "Have you thought about keeping those plants locked up?"

There was no answer at the phone number, so Shawn drove them all to the address. No one was home. All the way through that neighborhood the boys watched carefully out opposite sides of the car, looking for any sign of Stanley.

Michael said, "He has to be somewhere between where that lady saw him with the girl and the girl's house. But the police report said he kept up with her for several blocks, so we should look harder starting about halfway to her house."

Shawn slowly drove them along that way and back again. The houses in this part of town were big, set back from the road, spaced far apart, some with fences, hedges, or walls. Then they got out and walked, stopping to knock on doors to ask if anyone had seen anything. Few people were home. The ones they talked to had not seen the plant.

*　　*　　*

112

Finally Dad decided they should go home and keep trying to call the girl's house. Shawn drove back to their neighborhood and dropped off Dad, Mom, and Norman at the end of the street where it was blocked off. Michael rode back with him to the gas station to help reload his stuff.

After Shawn left on his interrupted trip, Michael told the attendant his family would be back that evening to pick up three of the bikes. He headed home, riding the one he had borrowed so he could return it and wondering if he would ever see Stanley again.

Chapter 17

After many attempts to call, Dad finally got an answer at the girl's house about eight-thirty that evening.

"Mr. Mason," Dad said, "I'm calling about the plant your daughter ran into today."

There was a long pause. Then the man replied suspiciously, "Are you from TV or the newspaper?"

"No," said Dad. "My son lost that plant when it got tangled up with a bicycle on the back of a car that towed it away."

"Is this some kind of a joke?" replied Mr. Mason grumpily.

"No," continued Dad. "We just need to ask your daughter where the plant was when she last saw it."

There was another long pause. "Is this one of those hidden camera shows that make people look like goofballs?"

"Certainly not," said Dad.

Mr. Mason said, "This better not be a setup for one of those nutsy programs. I won't have my family made fools of on TV!"

"No, we're just trying to find my son's plant! Really! If you don't believe me, call the police. They'll tell you we filed a missing plant report. That's where we got your name and number!''

"I'm not calling them again about this," said Mr. Mason. "When I talked to them before, they were laughing."

Dad said sympathetically, "They laughed at us, too."

Mr. Mason explained, "You can understand that we don't want any publicity about this. My daughter is upset enough already because on top of being chased by a plant, nobody believes her except me."

"We believe her," said Dad. "Could you just ask her where she escaped from it? All we need to know is where to start looking."

"Okay," agreed Mr. Mason. "I guess that plant should be gotten off the street before it goes after somebody else's child. Hang on a minute." Soon he came back on the phone. "Kristin doesn't know the names of the streets at the corner where she got away. She'll have to show you."

"Thanks," said Dad. "We've got your address. We'll be right over."

The whole family piled into the car. By now their street was no longer blocked off.

On the way they stopped at the gas station, thanked the attendant, and put the three remaining bikes in the trunk.

As they slowed up at the Masons' house, Dad observed, "It'll be dark soon."

Mom said, "I don't like to think about what might happen if Stanley is on the loose all night."

Norman suggested, "Maybe he's safe inside somebody's house."

"That could be even worse," said Mom.

Mr. Mason did not invite them in. After he looked

115

them over carefully and apparently decided they were not dangerous, he came out of his front door with Kristin, "We'll lead the way in our car," he said.

The Masons drove only a few blocks and then stopped at a corner where two streets crossed.

"It was right about here," said Kristin. "I looked back and it was farther behind me, not up close like before. Then I looked back one more time and it was gone."

"Gone where?" asked Michael. "Which way was it rolling?"

"I don't know," she replied. "It disappeared."

Michael recalled how Stanley had swung out behind him when they turned a corner for the parade.

"Did you turn a corner here?"

"No. But I did steer back and forth from one side of the street to the other a couple of times, trying to get away from it, because pedaling faster didn't work."

"Aha," said Michael. "Was the plant going back and forth, too?"

"Yeah, I could see it out of the sides of my eyes. Then it was gone. Like magic."

Michael said, "My plant wasn't really after you. It just got tangled up with your bike. It did it once before today." Kristin looked unconvinced.

Dad thanked the Masons, and they drove away.

The family all stood on the corner, looking around. Michael realized that Stanley must have swung out, let go of the bike, and rolled to a stop somewhere nearby. But where? In the gathering darkness lights had come on in a few houses set well back from the street. There were no curbs here or sidewalks, so Stanley could easily have kept rolling into one of these yards with lots of trees and hedges.

116

Dad and Norman went one way to look, and Mom and Michael went the other.

Michael said, "Stanley has to be around here somewhere close. Practically right under our noses. But I don't see him anywhere." Michael didn't want to think about the possibility, but Stanley could have gone a long way from here by hitching a ride on another bike.

He looked around at the dark outlines of trees all up and down the street. He remarked, "If there were a lot of big plants around here, Stanley could be blending in so we wouldn't notice him."

Mom said, "Trees are big plants. Let's look at them more closely. Stanley could probably masquerade as a short tree."

They checked every short tree up and down the road. None of them was Stanley. They also inspected a tall hedge that stood across the front of one property like a wide green wall.

Dad came up. "We've done all we can for tonight," he said. "In the morning we can call the police to see if they've had any found plants reported. And we can come back here and look some more and go door to door."

Michael sighed. He knew Dad was right, but he hated the idea of Stanley being lost, all alone and far from home—and with nothing to eat.

He sat down on the ground and started unlacing one sneaker. "If Stanley is around here," he said, "at least we can leave him something to eat. Everybody take off your socks!"

"Don't be silly," said Mom. "Where would we put them when we don't know where he is?"

"With four pairs of socks we can put them in eight

117

different places. Eight chances are better than nothing."
He took off one sock and put his shoe back on.

Mom said, "Oh, all right. Why not?" She sat down.
So did Dad and Norman.

Michael took off his other sock and put that shoe back on. He reached for the first sock he had tossed aside. It was not where he thought he'd left it.

He said to Norman, "Did you take my sock?"

"I wouldn't touch your stinky sock," replied Norman.

Then suddenly from behind them they heard a unexpected sound—"Schlurrrrrp."

Michael leaped up joyfully. "Stanley!" he called. "Where are you?"

"He must be in these bushes!" shouted Norman.

Mom said, "But none of these bushes is Stanley. We checked."

"I know how to find him now," said Michael. He held his other dirty sock out and started walking slowly along the hedge. A vine whipped out and grabbed the sock. Michael grabbed the vine and wrapped it around his waist.

"Hang on!" he said. He started walking toward the road, trying to tug the plant out. Dad ran around behind the hedge. "He's back here," Dad called, "with his wheels sunk in soft dirt. He must have been going really fast when he hit this hedge. He went right through it."

With Dad pushing and Michael pulling, Stanley popped out between the two huge bushes which had completely blocked him from view.

"Stanley," exclaimed Michael, "I'm so glad we found you! I was so worried!"

Stanley leaned against him, put a vine around his shoulder and burped.

* * *

Michael got his bike out of the trunk and carefully towed Stanley home, with the rest of the family following slowly in the car.

That night, after the boys had gone to sleep, Stanley's vines reached out to touch all the familiar objects in the room, as if to make sure he was safely home in the right place.

It was a hot night, so Michael had kicked his covers off. Toward morning, a chilly breeze blew in the open window. Michael shivered in his sleep, and Stanley gently pulled the covers up to his chin.

Chapter 18

The next day, when Mom came back from shopping, she was putting groceries away while the boys ate lunch. Norman was writing his initials on his food with the plastic squeeze bottle of ketchup.

"That reminds me," said Mom. "Have you cleaned the mustard out of your Blaster yet?"

"No," replied Norman. He was trying to make a cursive N, but it looked like just a red squiggle.

"Do it right after lunch," she said. "I don't want mustard leaking all over the house."

"Okay," agreed Norman. He licked the cursive N off his sandwich and started over.

"By the way," said Mom, "at the Save-A-Lot I saw Jason."

"What was he doing there?" asked Michael.

"Buying socks," she said.

Michael slammed his milk glass down. "What color socks?" he asked.

"Pink."

Norman exclaimed, "Strawberry!"

Mom looked appalled. "You don't think . . ." she began.

Michael said, "Jason would never wear pink socks."

Norman said, "But you said he said we got back all the plants and seeds."

Michael thought for a moment. "He said all the ones he *sold*. He wouldn't have had to sell one to himself. I'm going over there."

"Wait up!" yelled Norman. "I'm coming, too."

They rode their bikes across town to Jason's.

Norman asked, "What if nobody's home?"

Michael replied, "I'm trying to figure out what to say if he is home but doesn't invite us in. Or if he just lets us in as far as the living room."

Norman said, "I'll tell him I have to go to the bathroom. Then I can peek in the bedrooms on the way. And then I'll ask for a glass of water so I can go in the kitchen."

Michael wouldn't admit it, but he thought this was a good plan. He said, "Ask for the water first, and then the bathroom. That makes more sense."

When they arrived, Jason opened the door and said, "Hi." Now Michael had to think of what to say.

"Hi," he said. "I came over to show you my new bike. I got a great deal on it."

Jason came outside to look over the bike. Michael thought now it would be really awkward to try to get in the house.

But Norman was not shy. "I need to use your bathroom," he announced.

"Sure," said Jason. "Come on in."

After Norman went to the bathroom and checked the bedrooms, Jason's mother invited them into the kitchen for snacks. Then Jason took them to his room to show

121

them some computer games he had got a good deal on at a garage sale.

The only plants in the house were a few small ones in a kitchen window. Michael looked at them closely, but none resembled Stanley when he was a sprout.

By the time they left, Michael had given up on his suspicions. Maybe Jason had bought the pink socks for a present for someone. He did not realize that Jason had not taken them out in the backyard.

But even if he had, they would not have seen the plant, half as tall as Fluffy, which Jason was growing behind the garage.

0-595-32123-2

89275083R00073

Made in the USA
Middletown, DE
15 September 2018